Georgiana Marion Craik

Godfrey Helstone

A Novel: Vol.III.

Georgiana Marion Craik

Godfrey Helstone
A Novel: Vol.III.

ISBN/EAN: 9783337049980

Printed in Europe, USA, Canada, Australia, Japan

Cover: Foto ©Andreas Hilbeck / pixelio.de

More available books at **www.hansebooks.com**

GODFREY HELSTONE

A Novel

BY

GEORGIANA M. CRAIK

AUTHOR OF "TWO WOMEN," ETC.

IN THREE VOLUMES

VOL. III.

LONDON

RICHARD BENTLEY AND SON

Publishers in Ordinary to Her Majesty the Queen

1884

𝕷𝖔𝖓𝖌𝖆𝖞:

CLAY AND TAYLOR, PRINTERS.

GODFREY HELSTONE.

CHAPTER I.

GODFREY was in London one winter's night, two years after Margaret's death, and was making his way along the Strand through a dense fog, when, finding he had lost his bearings, he called to a man whose step he heard close to him "Can you tell me if I am near St. Martin's Church?" and, to his surprise, a familiar voice replied, "That's just what I am trying to find out for myself."

"You are Jack Dallas!" exclaimed Godfrey instantly.

"And — God bless me! — why, you're Helstone!" said the other.

And then the next moment with a hearty laugh they were shaking hands. It was a dozen years since they had seen each other last.

The hour was not a late one, and, when they had succeeded in discovering their position, Mr. Dallas made his friend go home with him, He had a comfortable bachelor establishment in rooms looking over the river.

"Married? Mercy on us, no!" he said in answer to an inquiry that Godfrey made. "I couldn't be married and go on living here, you know; and when a man has once got settled it needs a remarkably strong temptation to unsettle him again. At least that's my experience. I never have seen the temptation yet that would make me do

2

it ; and so, having reached my forty-fourth year without indulging in the blessing of a wife, I imagine the chances are that I shall go on in the same way to the end of the chapter."

"I think you are making a mistake, though," replied Godfrey.

He had told Jack already the bare fact that Margaret was dead. Presently, sitting with him over his fire, he spoke a little more of her, and of his daughter.

"I have been alone for two years now," he said, "and if it had not been for my little girl my life would be very empty. She was so quiet and retiring always that you must have lived with her to know how good she was. Of course *you* never knew her at all. That only time you came to us you were very little with her, I remember."

"No—ahem !—I didn't see a great deal

3

of her," assented Jack. "She—didn't seem to me to care for strangers."

"She was a very domestic woman," said Godfrey.

"Oh, yes — so I should suppose," responded Jack quickly. "I am sure she was—as good as she could be. She must have been a great loss to you."

"She has been a great loss to us both," said Godfrey. "To Rita as well as me."

"And how *is* Rita?" asked Jack. "Why, she must have grown out of all recollection!"

And then Godfrey replied with a laugh that he thought she probably had.

"She is a woman now," he said. "She will be eighteen next June."

"And she has forgotten my very name, I suppose?" said Mr. Dallas.

"Well," retorted Godfrey, "if she has, it is no one's fault but your own."

Godfrey had come to town for a week or two before Christmas. He wanted some books, he told Mr. Dallas.

"I can't think why in the world you don't come up oftener," Jack replied. "I like the country myself—in moderation—as much as any man; but as for living in it all the year round—unless you are compelled, I think it is an utter mistake. What in the world makes *you* do it is more than I can conceive."

"Oh, I am generally up in town every year," Godfrey said in self-defence.

"Yes; you come for a flying visit like this. What is the good of flying visits? You ought to spend half the year here. That is what I would do if I were in your place. But prosperity has made a Sybarite

5

of you, I'm afraid. You want a big house always to live in. You can't do without your carriages and your horses and your half-score of servants."

"I could do with a garret and a dry crust, if it came to that," exclaimed Godfrey rather indignantly.

"Oh, well, that is going beyond *me*," replied Jack. "A lodging like this is all I had in my mind; and I say again, you might do worse—indeed, I don't know that you could do much better—than pitch your tent in a place of this sort for a good portion, at any rate, of every year."

"And leave Rita at Ivor?" asked Godfrey.

"Oh, bless me, I quite forgot Rita!" exclaimed Mr. Dallas.

Upon which his companion laughed. "She

is not quite so important a person, you see, to you as she is to me," he said.

"I find that most of the schemes we make in life get knocked on the head," said Jack philosophically. "Well, you must wait till the girl takes a husband. She will be doing that, I suppose, before long."

"I don't know," replied Godfrey rather quickly. "I hope she won't be doing it yet."

"Well, they mostly do. They either marry, or they give more trouble with their lovers than if they did. It's best to get them well off your hands at once, I believe. Near eighteen—did you say she was? Oh, then, she will be in the thick of it immediately. It's about as bad an age as you could choose."

"I hope you will prove a false prophet," said Godfrey, not feeling comfortable, however. "I shall be sorry, for my own part, if she leaves me before she is five-and-twenty."

"Oh, of course you will miss her whenever she goes," said Jack. "That's the worst of marrying and having children. You are always getting stabbed in one direction or another. I don't think I could stand it, for my own part. She's a pretty little thing now, I suppose?"

"She isn't little," responded Godfrey. "She is five feet six. I dare say you would think her pretty. Most people do."

"And her father agrees with them?'" said Jack with a kindly laugh. "Well, I should like to come and have a look at her again. I would come after Christmas, I am half disposed to think, if you cared to ask me."

"Change your time a little, and come before Christmas," answered Godfrey.

"Why shouldn't you? Come home with me on the 16th."

"What, next Friday? Oh, I hardly think I could do that," said Jack.

But five minutes afterwards he had agreed to do it.

"Papa is going to bring somebody back with him," said Rita to her quondam governess, Miss Taylor, reading a letter that she had from her father a day or two after this. "A Mr. Dallas. I remember he was here once before, ever so long ago. And papa says, would you please get a room ready for him, as he is coming to stay over Christmas. Oh, dear," said Rita with a little sigh, "I am rather sorry that anybody who is old is coming for Christmas."

"Is he old?" replied Miss Taylor innocently. "Oh, but you know some old people are very nice. Let us hope that

Mr. Dallas will be. I think we will give him the green room, dear. It is the best for an elderly person. It is so nice and warm."

So then Miss Taylor had the green room prepared, and kept a good fire burning in it for two days before Mr. Dallas arrived. The old gentleman might perhaps have rheumatism, or asthma, she thought.

It was mild weather, but with considerate kindness Miss Taylor sent a closed carriage to the station to meet the travellers.

"Why didn't you bring the dog-cart?" Godfrey asked his servant, when he found this equipage waiting for them; but the man answered that he had only done as he was told.

"Oh yes, of course; they know your tastes. Didn't I say that you lived in the lap of luxury?" exclaimed Jack, and he chuckled mischievously as he took his comfortable seat. He rather enjoyed chaffing Godfrey and crediting him with a love of ease that he, for his own part, professed to scorn.

There was an open door to receive them at their journey's end, and a warm glow of lamp and fire-light in the hall, and in the midst of the glow Rita's girlish figure.

"That looks pretty," said Jack, gazing at the picture as the carriage drove up.

In another moment or two he had jumped out and was upon the door-step looking on while Rita kissed her father.

"Ah, you don't remember *me*?" he said when that ceremony was concluded, and then he put out his hand, and, looking demure and pretty, Rita took it.

"No, I don't remember you," she answered.

"This is my friend Mr. Dallas, Miss

11

Taylor," Godfrey announced; and Miss Taylor found herself gazing in surprise at the youthful-looking man who turned and greeted her.

"Why, I quite misunderstood. Rita said he was *old*," she exclaimed to Godfrey afterwards. "I got the warmest room in the house ready for him, and sent the close carriage to meet you."

Godfrey burst out laughing. "That is too good a joke not to be told to Jack," he said; and so presently he turned the tables on his friend with some enjoyment.

"Rita expected you to arrive upon crutches," he said. "No wonder Miss Taylor sent an easy carriage for you. She has been making all kinds of preparations for your comfort. You will find the softest easy-chair in your room, and there will be hot water bottles in your bed presently."

12

"Hm! and so that is how youth would treat a decent middle age!" exclaimed Jack, not condescending after this speech to more than a smile.

"Now I drew a much truer picture of *you*," he said to Rita in the course of the evening. "I knew exactly what you would be like. When I last had the pleasure of seeing you, you were a small person in pinafores. You had your hair cropped all round your head. You had a habit of screwing your knuckles into your eyes, and of occasionally howling, and you used to sit on my knee and play with my watch-chain. I was prepared to find you very much changed, but I knew exactly the amount of change there would be. I knew you would appear with your hair turned up, and your pinafores gone, and your frocks down to your heels; but I never expected

13

to find you transformed into a matronly woman, with wrinkles on your brow. See how much common sense I have, and how wanting in common sense *you* must be!"

And then he stood rather defiantly before her and laughed; and Rita was a little abashed, and did not quite know what to say.

It was true she had called him old, and as far as years went he *was* old, she thought, and yet she could not but allow to herself that he certainly had not the look or manner of an elderly gentleman.

"I was so little when I saw you before; you forget that," she said rather deprecatingly after a moment.

"And I seemed so very big, do you mean to imply?" he asked.

"N-o; you are not so very big." Rita said this a little bluntly. "I don't suppose

14

I ever thought you that; but I am sure you know," half reproachfully, "that when one is a child *all* grown up people seem rather old."

"And how do they seem," inquired Jack pleasantly, "when one comes to be, let us say, eighteen or thereabouts?"

And then poor Rita looked embarrassed, and blushed again.

"I don't know," she said shyly.

"I suppose you still think of me as a sort of Methuselah?"

"No, I don't," she said.

"One of the patriarchs then, at any rate?"

"I think you look younger than papa does," she said.

"Well, I ought to, for I am his junior by three months, and at our time of life three months tell," replied Jack gravely.

15

"Are you and papa really so near the same age?" she asked. "I should hardly have guessed that. Papa is so much graver than you are."

"He has had such a comfortable life, that's the reason of it," replied Jack with a confident air. "Nothing makes one so grave as prosperity. It's a curious thing, you know. You feel yourself such an example when it comes upon you, as if all the world were looking at you. But when you get knocked about like a football, and know that nobody is looking at you, why then you can keep hold of your youth, and remain a boy just as long as you please. I've never been embarrassed by being looked at myself," said Jack modestly, "and so I'm glad to say I've kept up my spirits amazingly."

"Papa," said Rita, rather severely, later

in the evening, to her father, " I think that Mr. Dallas talks sometimes in a very foolish way."

Rita was certainly more puzzled than pleased with her visitor on this first evening of his stay with them. She did not know when he was jesting and when he was serious ; he seemed to her to be rather frequently engaged in laughing at her, and she had a good deal of self-esteem, and by no means liked to be laughed at. After he had talked to her for a little while she got out of his way, and gave him no more opportunity than she could help of talking to her again.

" I don't like people who are always making fun," she said. " He isn't nearly so old as I supposed he was, but if he were really older I think perhaps I should like him better." And so she went to bed in no especial charity with her new friend.

But Jack was one of those people who, by their abounding good humour and absence of self-consciousness, soften adverse opinions, and as the next day passed Rita began, half-involuntarily, to think that there were some rather pleasant things in him at any rate. She met him, to begin with, the first thing in the morning, coming in, though it was December, from an early ramble in the garden, with a little robin in his hand that he had picked up from the ground.

"Come here," he said, calling to her as he entered the house. "I wonder what you can do for this little beggar?" And then he showed his small captive to her, and roused her in a moment to interest and sympathy.

18

"Oh, what is the matter with him? Do you think we can keep him alive?" she exclaimed.

"You can but try at any rate, I suppose," he said. "He isn't worth the trouble, but you must either do that or wring his neck. I'll wring his neck in a moment, if you think that will be the best way of dealing with him."

But of course Rita thought nothing of the sort, and set down Jack as little better than a heathen for proposing such a course.

"Then get something to put him in," he said.

So she hurried away, and found a little empty cage, and they made a bed, and laid the bird in it.

"He seems to have something the matter with his feet. Look at him, poor little chap, he can't stand for a moment on them.

19

Do you know now what I would advise you to do?" said Jack. "I would get a little sherry and put his legs into it."

"Are you saying that in joke?" asked Rita, looking solemnly at him.

"In joke? Not I!" cried Jack. "I had a cousin once who cured her canary so. The canary's legs gave way, just like these, and she gave him wine baths till she brought him round, and he got as merry as a grig again. Just let us have a little wine and some warm water, and we'll bathe this fellow." And then Rita got the wine, and they gave their patient his bath.

It was very kind of him, Rita thought. She had not supposed he would have been so kind.

"We shall have to go through the business two or three times a day," he said, "if we mean to do any good by it; but you will scarcely care to take all that trouble perhaps?"

"*I* not care? Oh yes, I shall," cried Rita quickly. And then she thought it behoved her to say something more, and she added rather shyly—"Thank you very much for having shown me how to do it."

"Then you propose to do without my help in future—do you?" asked Jack instantly. "Oh come, that won't do. The bird's mine."

"But—but—" said Rita, and then suddenly stopped and burst out laughing. How could he talk in such a boyish way? she wondered. "What a thing to say!" she exclaimed. "As if you could want him!"

"Why shouldn't I want him? I'm very fond of birds. I don't see the fun," replied Jack with such gravity that Rita checked

21

herself and felt ashamed. He must be very simple-minded to care so much about a robin at his time of life, she thought.

However, the discovery of so innocent a predilection in him, though it seemed to her very odd, decidedly had the effect of rather inclining her in his favour. She gave him breakfast after this, and put an extra lump of sugar in his cup of coffee, with a half-conscious intention of pandering to his juvenile tastes. She offered him jam, and felt pleased when she saw him eat it. "He says he is as old as you are. Papa, is he really so old?" she said to her father in a tone of amazement presently, at a time when Jack's back was turned.

The sun was shining, and for December it was a pleasant day. They all three went out to ride in the course of the morning. Rita and Godfrey at most times

22

were in the habit of riding a great deal
together, and usually on these occasions
they talked a great deal together too; but
to-day Jack's presence kept Rita silent, and
she only, for the most part, cantered by her
father's side, and listened while the other
two recalled old days and spoke of old
companions. Their talk concerned itself
with a time that seemed to her as if it
must be very far away,—with events that
had happened before her own birth; but
she listened to it and was interested. She
had often before now been told stories by
her father of his early life, but to-day,
both by him and Mr. Dallas she heard
certain names mentioned familiarly for the
first time.

"Who were the Beresfords, papa?" she
asked after a little while, in a tone that
she only meant for her father's ears.

"They were a family that Mr. Dallas and I knew one summer," Godfrey replied. "A clergyman's family in Derbyshire."

"I never remember your speaking of them before. You seem to have known them very well," said Rita.

And then he made no answer. He merely turned his head, and said something again to Jack.

"You're a capital rider," Mr. Dallas remarked abruptly to Rita as they were nearing home. "Now I think it's a nice thing for a girl to ride well. It isn't only that it's a pretty thing, but it trains a woman; it gives her nerve, and braces her up altogether. You see, you can't be a good horsewoman and a coward at the same time, can you?"

"I suppose not—in some ways," said Rita.

24

"No, of course you can't; it stands to reason," exclaimed Jack insistently. "No coward ever was at home on a horse. You wouldn't be afraid now of an animal with some spirit in him, I should say? I don't for my own part when I ride look out for a beast with spirit," said Mr. Dallas with his usual openness; "it would be very bad both for the beast and for me I am afraid if I did; but then, you see, I'm a towns-man, and that makes a difference, doesn't it? I hardly find myself on a horse once in a twelvemonth."

"Oh," said Rita, "I shouldn't like that!"

"No, I don't suppose you would. And perhaps I shouldn't like to live here, and have to ride every day. It may strike you as odd, Miss Rita, but I am afraid I should find it monotonous. Just consider—three hundred and sixty-five days in a year, or

25

three hundred and thirteen, if you strike off the Sundays, and only perhaps a dozen different roads to ride on! Now life with us in London isn't like that. It's capable of infinite varieties. Here is your father who knows it is, though he thinks it best to hold his tongue. I was telling him the other day to come to town and stop there."

"Oh!" cried Rita with a little gasp.

"What does that 'oh!' mean?" asked Jack. "Do you think you wouldn't like it? Ah, but you would, take my word for that. You would like it amazingly. Everybody does who tries it long enough. At this distance from London it's my belief that nobody ever does anything worth doing."

"And how many in London either do what is worth doing?" asked Godfrey, with rather a bitter laugh.

26

"Well, I hold that the proportion of those who do something, at any rate, is greater," said Jack. "Take myself, if you like, as an instance. Why, when I'm in town I gird up my loins and work; but if I lived here I should be like those cows there, and lie in a field all day and ruminate. I think it's delightful to be in a field, ruminating,—now and then, but as to passing the main part of one's life in that condition—"

"But we don't!" interrupted Rita with the colour in her face.

And then Jack bowed, and with an inward chuckle, suddenly held his peace.

"Miss Rita, do you sing?" he asked his young hostess that same afternoon, and, when she answered that she sang a little, he made her go to the piano, and sing pretty near a dozen songs to him. He

27

sat meanwhile in a comfortable arm-chair, and gazed complacently into the fire. " I like this," he said once. Miss Taylor sitting at her work-table thought him a man of rather idle tastes perhaps. As for Rita—well, if he liked her singing Rita naturally was pleased.

The entertainment went on for nearly an hour, and only once, as Rita touched the opening notes of a certain old French song, did Mr. Dallas disturb himself even for a moment in his lazy enjoyment. On this single occasion, however, he raised his head abruptly from its cushioned repose, and looked quickly round at Rita.

" Where did you get that ? That's one of Joanne Beresford's songs," he said.

" One of—one of those Beresfords' you were talking of this morning ? " asked Rita surprised.

"Yes; Joanne Beresford's. I've heard her sing it a dozen times. Where did you get it from?"

"I have it in a book of old French music," Rita said. "Papa used not to like it, I think. At least—" she said, and stopped abruptly.

"Oh, your father liked it," cried Jack. "In those old days he liked it amazingly. I was sick of hearing him croaking it. Ah, she sang wonderfully, that girl. She had a real genius. Queer, to come across one of her songs again!" And Jack recushioned his head on its pillow, and laughed a little softly as he resigned himself once more to his idle listening.

But Rita, she was not quite sure why, did not resume the prelude she had begun. She struck a chord or two, and then passed into another key, wondering a little, and questioning something that she would have liked, if she had been less shy, to put into words; and Joanne Beresford's song would not have been sung at all if Jack had not interposed again. When he heard her turning to another air, however, he stopped her.

"But you haven't given me that one," he said.

"N—o," answered Rita dubiously. "I think, if you used to hear it very well sung, I had better not."

"Oh, now that's nonsense!" exclaimed Jack. "I sha'n't compare you with Miss Joanne. And besides, if I did, it wouldn't matter,—and I want to hear the old song again; I do indeed."

So then Rita said no more, but sang it.

She did not sing it as Joanne Beresford

had been used to do, yet Jack liked her performance very well. Joanne's singing had never been to him what it had been to Godfrey.

"The sound of that makes me feel twenty years younger," he said when Rita had ended the quaint old air. But he made no other remark, and Rita made none.

"Do you know that Mr. Dallas sings himself?" Godfrey asked his daughter, coming presently into the room; and Rita at this question opened her eyes.

"Mr. Dallas? *Does* he?" she exclaimed in a tone that made Jack laugh.

"My dear Miss Helstone," he said, "I used to sing once, but since I have been toothless—"

"You are *not* toothless," she interrupted him, knitting her brows. "I can't think

31

why you say such things. Please sing something,—if you do sing," and then her tone softened and became rather apologetic. "I should like to hear you very much."

But Jack shook his head. "I doubt if my asthma will let me," he said gravely, and Rita would not have known if he was speaking in earnest or jest if her father had not laughed.

"Suppose you try, without regard to your asthma," he advised.

And then, with a groan of dissatisfaction, Jack rose from his comfortable chair, and went to the piano, and sang with a freshness and animation that almost took Rita's breath away. He sang a hunting song, and a fighting song, and after that he sang a love song; but at the end of this third effort he suddenly feigned to be affected with an attack of coughing, and rose up from the music-stool with an air of decrepitude that for a moment or two at any rate quite took Rita in.

"Oh, I am so sorry!" she exclaimed anxiously, thinking that out of courtesy he had exerted himself beyond his strength, and, if her face had not proved too much for his gravity, she would probably have added some farther expressions of distress. He saved her from this, however, by giving way to a burst of laughter.

"Miss Rita, you make me ashamed to play tricks upon you!" he exclaimed next moment. "You oughtn't to be so kind to me. If I wear out your pity on false pretences perhaps there will be none of it left to give me when I really need it."

"I think you laugh at me very much,"

she answered, rather reproachfully. "I shall try not to be taken in again."

"Oh, I hope you won't do that!" cried Jack.

He had already said to Godfrey, "She is so delightfully simple. I haven't come across such an unsophisticated girl for years. A dear little soul, and a pretty little soul too. I like her immensely. Now, if I had married, that is the sort of daughter I should have wanted to have." And Godfrey had liked this flattery; what father would not?

"She is a good girl," he had merely answered, but his heart had responded gratefully to Jack's praise. He even himself approved the more of Rita because she pleased his friend. He looked at her with critical eyes when he saw her next, and told himself contentedly that she was worth looking at. A dainty little girl, with a pure sweet face. Many a girl might be both prettier and cleverer, but Rita was good enough to satisfy him,—or almost any man, he thought.

CHAPTER II.

"I am afraid the little bird is not better," Rita had said to Jack when they came home from their ride, and Mr. Dallas had visited the patient with her, and when lunch was over, before Rita began to sing, they had administered another bath to him. But perhaps Mr. Dallas's system of cure was not one adapted to the robin's case, for an hour or two later in the afternoon Rita came in search of Jack, with the cage in her hand, and a pathetic look in her face.

"Oh, Mr. Dallas," she exclaimed, "he is dead!"

Jack took the bird, and deliberately surveyed it.

"Ungrateful little chap!" he said. "A better bird would have tried to live, if only to show his sense of what we have been doing for him. Well, it can't be helped. He's gone his own way now. Give me a shovel, and I'll get him buried."

"*I* had been going to bury him. I needn't trouble you," Rita answered hesitatingly a little; but he shook his head.

"My aged limbs will carry me as far as the garden," he said. "Come with me, if you like, though, and see where I put him. At a funeral there should always be one mourner at least, as well as the grave-digger."

So then they went out together in the

37

twilight into the garden, and buried the robin under a tree.

"We wasted a glass of good sherry on him," said Jack, when the ceremony was ended. "I am afraid it was more than he was worth."

"But it was kind of you to try and cure him," said Rita quickly. "I think it was very good-natured. So many people would not have cared."

"Oh, I did it out of idleness," exclaimed Jack. "I don't suppose it was a right thing to do. Idle hands, you know, Dr. Watts says, only move in the service of the devil. You believe in Dr. Watts, Miss Rita, don't you?"

"I don't quite know what you mean by——believing in him," answered Rita a little embarrassed. "I think some of the hymns he wrote are very nice."

38

"So they are. They're admirable!" exclaimed Jack with fervour. "I used to have scores of them in my head once, and the few I have retained through life have been of the utmost service to me. Especially those lines about the devil and idle hands. I have found occasion to repeat them many hundreds of times."

"But is it any good—merely to repeat them?" asked Rita gravely.

"Well, at any rate it must be better than *not* to repeat them, mustn't it?" said Jack. "You'll allow that, surely? Come, you *must* allow that?"

And then Rita, confused, did not know what answer to make. She was clearly not quite at ease with Mr. Dallas, nor did she understand nor quite approve of his manner of talking. But her perplexity seemed to amuse her companion, for his eyes filled with laughter whem she was silent, and then after a moment or two:

"I see how it is," he exclaimed,—"like all young people you are hard upon the weaknesses of old age. It is all very well to be told you are never to have idle hands in youth, but Dr. Watts himself could never have meant to apply his precept to a time when your hands are getting cramped with rheumatism."

"Are *your* hands getting cramped with rheumatism? I am sure they are not," said Rita severely.

"My dear Miss Helstone," replied Jack in his pleasantest tone, "is it not the truest wisdom to prepare ourselves beforehand for the infirmities that in the course of nature will come upon us? Ah, that is one way in which we of a mature age have greatly the advantage of you: we look ahead; we recognize that life is passing ; we adapt ourselves to circumstances. I think, for my own part, that, excellent as they are, Dr. Watts's hymns show' signs of being written by an *im*mature mind, and by a mind without true sympathy for age. I wouldn't say so to everybody, but upon my word I do."

" Are you always laughing at people ? " asked Rita after a moment's silence.

"I ?" exclaimed Jack innocently. " Bless you, no ! What in the world made you think that ? Oh dear, no : I am a very grave person. I take life very sadly for the most part. It is from you and people of your standing that I look for laughter. If I have a fault to find with you indeed, Miss Rita—if I may venture to find a fault it is that I haven't as yet heard you laugh enough."

It was dark outside, but they had re-entered the house by this time, and Jack had placed himself in front of the hall fire which was burning brightly, and throwing out a warm glow on the pictured walls. The evening was not a cold one, but still the fire was pleasant, and Jack standing upon the heathrug seemed to enjoy his position.

"I laugh a great deal," replied Rita rather shyly. "Of course, when you are strange to people, you don't laugh before them so much."

"Well that is all right," said Jack approvingly. "I like not to have the best of a thing at first. You see, if I tell you the truth, I am an Epicurean, and I think it is the best wisdom to take my pleasures deliberately,—to taste them bit by bit, not to gulp them whole. Now, of course, *you* are not an Epicurean at all in that sense.

42

Nobody is at your age. You like to seize the whole of everything at once."

But at this Rita shook her head.

"I don't think I do," she said.

"Oh, you may fancy you don't, but you do probably all the same," persisted Jack. "Everybody does when they are young, more or less. You need age and wisdom to lead you to the other way. That is a grave truth, Miss Rita, though you look as if you weren't willing to receive it."

"I suppose you are speaking seriously now, but I am not quite sure," said Rita, looking at him dubiously.

"Most certainly I am speaking seriously. I nearly always speak seriously," declared Jack with boldness. "You seem somehow to have taken up the notion that I jest a great deal, but I am afraid the error is in yourself, and that you sometimes mistake my wisdom for folly."

And then she laughed. He seemed to her very odd, but she was beginning to have rather a kindly feeling to him in spite of his oddness.

"I think," said Miss Taylor later in the evening, "that Mr. Dallas does himself injustice by his manner. There is more in him than you would suppose at first. He seems so very light and almost boyish on the surface, but if you once get him to talk gravely he has a great deal of good sense."

"Yes, that must be so, of course, or else papa wouldn't like him," answered Rita.

But still, as far as she personally was concerned, it was mainly the boyish side of himself that Mr. Dallas had as yet shown to her.

44

She saw more of him as the days went on, and got perhaps to understand him a little better. He and Godfrey used to spend a great deal of their time together. As these days passed they renewed their former intimacy, and perhaps even drew the cords of their friendship closer than they had been drawn of old. Jack took to the life at Ivor very kindly. He professed to be wholly a townsman, but he showed a very fair appreciation of the pleasures of the country; he laughed at Godfrey for what he chose to call his love of luxury, but he was by no means slow to enjoy such luxuries as were offered to himself. "Upon my word, you lead a pleasant life!" he told his friend with warmth before more than a week of his visit had expired.

Perhaps to Mr. Dallas it did not seem

that Margaret's death had left much sense of vacancy in the household. For his own part he did not miss her. As far as he was concerned, Miss Taylor, who was always ladylike and agreeable, filled, and even more than filled, the place that she had left. "Godfrey had a sad loss when his wife died," Mrs. Helstone said to him one day, and Jack of course looked grave, and tried to make some sympathetic response, but the sentence he uttered was rather feeble and commonplace.

"Yes—your acquaintance with her was so slight that you could not know her worth," Mrs. Helstone went on. "She was one of those women whom you needed to know well to appreciate. No one ever had a more unselfish nature. Not many can ever have had fewer faults."

"Ah—so I should think. She certainly seemed—wonderfully free from anything of that sort," Jack murmured, not very felicitously.

He was thinking while he spoke that, in spite of her virtues, it must have been a strange kind of living death to have been tied to her. "Perhaps she suited him," he meditated. "There is no saying what sort of woman may suit any man, but I think if the case had been mine—"

And then he glanced round the handsome room in which he was sitting, and wondered if he would have been tempted—as Godfrey had been tempted, he supposed. For he had settled his theory of Godfrey's marriage long ago, making up his mind about it as most people on the evidence that he possessed would have done. The case to him had always been as clear as daylight.

47

He could come to no other conclusion than that except for her money he would never have married Margaret Egerton and have left Joanne Beresford alone.

And yet, after having retained this belief for almost twenty years, one day during these weeks he suddenly became shaken in it, for, happening on this occasion to say something about the Beresfords, and that abrupt journey of the Vicar and his daughter to town, Godfrey—unconsciously, in all likelihood, at the moment—betrayed a knowledge of Joanne's lengthened stay in London that made Jack in surprise prick up his ears.

"How do you know that she stayed long in town?" he asked quickly.

And then Godfrey hesitated for a moment, but after that moment quietly replied—"Because I saw her there."

"Bless me!" exclaimed Jack. "You never told me."

"I had no reason to tell you," Godfrey answered gravely. "I saw her one day at her aunt's house; that was all."

Whereupon Jack ejaculated "Oh!" and then abruptly held his peace.

But this unexpected morsel of information that he had gained set Mr. Dallas's wits to work, and led him to form a new conception of the circumstances that had induced his friend to become the husband of Miss Egerton.

"He must have asked Joanne and been refused by her," he thought. "Ten to one he asked her that day he speaks of, and only fell back on the other girl when she wouldn't have him. Poor old boy! If that is the true story it has been rather hard lines for him. But yet, hard lines or not," added Jack heartily, "I'm glad he tried to get the right girl before he took the other; upon my word I am."

And, in truth, a warmer feeling for Godfrey sprang up in his heart than had been there for many a day, for, though he had liked him always, he had also, ever since his former visit to Ivor, felt a certain contempt for him for having sold himself, as he believed he had done, to Margaret Egerton. He had thought that, with many good qualities, he must be a worldly fellow at bottom; but now he said to himself that, if indeed Joanne Beresford had refused him, Godfrey's marriage with his cousin had been a natural and quite an excusable event. "For if a man can't get the best thing, he is wisest to put up with the second best," he thought,

50

"and be content, if he can, with the goods the gods provide him. Helstone has had a prosperous life—whatever he may have missed; and he has got a dear little daughter now. Yes, a dear little soul,— bless her. I wish I had anything belonging to me in the world that was half so sweet."

And then Jack gave a half-envious sigh. He was a man who on the whole took life very lightly, yet he had his grave and even his sad moments, and in some of these he was pretty keenly conscious that his existence was a lonely and rather purposeless one. Godfrey was richer and happier than he was, he thought, even though he might have failed to marry the woman that he loved.

Yet, in spite of such occasional grave reflections, Mr. Dallas much enjoyed his

Christmas holiday. It was the pleasantest holiday, he told Rita, that he had known for years.

"Yes, the weather is so nice," Rita answered when he said this.

And then Jack assented, and agreed that the weather was charming, but yet he was conscious enough that the secret of his enjoyment did not lie only in the fairness and mildness of the days. He liked the life altogether that he found his friends leading: he liked his talks and walks with Godfrey: he liked the sight of Rita's bright face.

"I wish I had been like you, and married twenty years ago," he said to Godfrey once. "Only, if I had, instead of a single girl, I should probably have had half-a-dozen boys who would have pestered the life out of me. That was what I was always afraid of whenever I thought of the business seriously. I couldn't have stood half-a-dozen boys."

"Oh, there are worse things than that," answered Godfrey with suavity. "I should have liked very well to have a boy."

"You might have liked to have *one* boy, but do you mean to say that you think you would have liked to have *six* boys?" retorted Jack indignantly. "And even with regard to one, what good would there have been in it? You are far better with nobody but Rita. Rita is perfect by herself. If she had had a brother she might have been a tom-boy."

"Well, I am content enough with her," said Godfrey with a laugh.

It had always been Mr. Helstone's habit to have his daughter a great deal in his study with him. Rita was not a student,

but in a light desultory way she was
fond of reading, and Godfrey liked nothing
better than to have her read beside him.
In winter especially they used to spend
half their time in his room together—he
at his table, she coiled into an arm-chair
near the fire. Here she would read, and
hence she would chatter. Her father's
habits of work had to a considerable ex-
tent trained her to silence, so that she
was used to keep her tongue at rest as
long as he sat before his desk or held
his pen, but he had only to rise from his
seat to loose that vivacious member from
its bonds. She was one of those little
maidens who always have something on
their lips that they want to say — whose
simple minds are like a full measure run-
ning over. For Rita was not particularly
clever, but she loved to talk. She liked

54

to talk and to be talked to; she was not fond of silence or sadness.

She was a little shy at first of coming to her usual place in the library after Mr. Dallas's arrival, but when a couple of days had passed her father made some remark about her absence in Jack's hearing, which had the effect of restoring the customary order of things.

"You don't mean to say that you have been keeping out of your father's room on my account? Oh, come," cried Mr. Dallas vehemently, "if you do that, I shall have to go back to town."

So then Rita was obliged to say that she would not do it; and indeed she was pleased enough to return to her cosy corner.

"I thought perhaps Mr. Dallas would find it stupid to have me so much here,"

55

she said doubtfully to her father, but he gave a laugh and quieted her scruples.

"My dear, Mr. Dallas is not shy," he told her. "He is fond of an audience. If he were to begin to seek retirement now he would be doing it for the first time in his life."

And indeed Jack for himself made no profession of desiring to seek retirement. He was a genial man who liked company. He had no objection, but quite the reverse, to talk in Rita's hearing. Very soon he got enough liking for her to feel a sense of pleasure in the consciousness that she was listening when he held forth, and that her bright young eyes were often turned upon his face. Indeed, before long, he even directed no small part of his conversation to her. "She is such a dear little soul," he declared repeatedly to Godfrey, and Godfrey liked his appreciation and his praise.

In this winter weather they naturally spent a large portion of their time in-doors, and Jack liked no part of the house so well as that comfortable library of Godfrey's. Here round the ample fire Godfrey and he and Rita often sat together. Godfrey in these days did no work, but he was content to read and enjoy his friend's society. And Rita, too, for her part, read and talked, and gradually got to know more of Jack, and sometimes to like him better,—sometimes not to be sure whether she liked him or not.

For, to tell the truth, Jack did not always treat her well. He used at times to forget the dignity of her—almost—eighteen years, and would tease her, and laugh at her, and try to make her angry by professing opinions on various subjects that seemed very mistaken, and sometimes very terrible, opinions to her. He used to puzzle her too by frequently leaving her in the dark as to whether he was in earnest or not.

"I am sure you say a great many things that you never mean at all," she told him reproachfully one day. "I can't think how you can feel it right to do that. If anybody who was young did so—" And then she stopped, not liking to carry her sentence to its natural severe issue.

But Jack had no scruples, and finished it in the pleasantest way.

"If anybody who was young did it, he'd be whipped—wouldn't he?" he said. "That's what I should tell any boy of mine who told lies. But, my dear Miss Rita, *I* am *not* young, you see, and one of the privileges of age is that it is not whipped for lying. I was a model of veracity when I was a lad. I was, I assure you."

"And now do you mean that you are not?" asked Rita sternly.

Whereupon Jack put on a pathetic face, and gazed at her so sadly that, though she felt convinced of his guilt, she had not the heart to continue her rebuke. "I am afraid he is not very good," she only thought gravely to herself presently; "and I wish he was, for I think he is nice. I do wish he wouldn't say so many things that seem wrong." But still, perhaps just because he did this, and she was so sorry for him, Rita used to listen to his talk a great deal, and felt pleased when he talked as she liked him to talk, and grieved when he disappointed her and said things of which she disapproved.

"He does really pretend a great deal—doesn't he, papa?" she asked Godfrey once, and it made her glad when her father answered with a laugh that undoubtedly he pretended very much indeed.

"He likes to tease you, because he sees that you don't understand him," he said.

And then Rita meditated for a moment or two, and presently softly stroked her father's hand.

"I am glad *you* don't tease me, and make me misunderstand," she said, with a loving look into his eyes.

They used to ride together, and walk together, and sing together, and in short to be more together than apart. It is so easy to grow into new habits, and before Jack had been ten days at Ivor, Rita would have missed him if he had gone away.

One morning in the second week of his stay he said something about the end of his visit being near, and the girl gave a little quick ejaculation. "Oh, no!" she exclaimed; "you have only just come. I thought you were going to stay a long time?"

"Well, I *am* staying a long time," Jack answered. "A fortnight in one house, I consider, is a very long time."

"I think if you say that you must be tired," said Rita.

And then Jack answered very warmly that he was by no means tired. "I like being here immensely," he told her. "I don't know when I have enjoyed anything so much. But I must go home to work, you know."

"I thought you had no work to do just now?" said Rita doubtfully.

At that he laughed. "See what comes of living with an idle man! Do you think that all people are like your father?"

"Papa is not idle," answered Rita rebukingly. "You can't think how hard he often works. I don't know what you mean by saying I live with an idle man."

"Oh, well, I cry *Peccavi!* I will alter my expression, and say that you live with a man of leisure. Come, you can't object to my putting it so. Your father hasn't got to earn his bread."

"No," said Rita, but she made the admission rather reluctantly. "He doesn't earn his bread; but he works," she added obstinately.

"And I work and earn my bread both," said Jack.

And then for a moment or two she made no answer.

"But it isn't very difficult for you—is it?" she asked abruptly after that little silence. "I mean, I suppose as you are not married you don't need to work very hard?"

"Ah, I don't know about that. It takes a good deal to keep me," said Jack. "It always does take a good deal to keep a bachelor, I am told. Yes—you are wrong: I do work hard. I strongly suspect I should come upon the parish if I didn't."

"Then I am afraid you don't manage well," said Rita gravely.

"Why of course I don't manage well!" cried Jack. "Is it likely that I should? I am pillaged right and left. That's inevitable."

"I am very sorry," said Rita with concern.

"Well, I am sorry too,—but of course that trouble is only in the nature of things. I never think about it. If I earn enough to pay my landlady, and to supply myself with my few little comforts,—my stall at the opera, you know, and my hansom, and my valet, and so on (I don't spend above five or six hundred a year on these trifles) —if I can earn, I say, enough to make both ends meet in my modest way, that is all I care about. I never was dependent on luxuries—like your father, you know."

"How can you say that papa is dependent on luxuries?" cried Rita, with the colour coming hotly into her face. "I don't believe you can have lived here even for these few days without knowing better than that; and I am sure, if you talk of spending all that money on your 'comforts,' that you must care far more—ten times more— But

64

I don't believe that you really have a stall at the opera? and—those other things?" she suddenly exclaimed, interrupting her sentence, and looking half-inquiringly, half-deprecatingly into his face.

He began to chuckle and rub his hands together.

"I keep a tame leopard at my lodgings, and smoke my pipe in an eastern robe, sitting cross-legged on a divan," he said. "In these days a man must do something to separate him from the common herd."

"And *you* do that by saying things that are not true," she told him indignantly.

Upon which, I am ashamed to say, at first he only laughed, though presently he begged her to forgive him.

"For, you know, when people live alone they get into such bad habits," he said. "They lose all the virtues that civilization teaches them,—truth, and kindness, and belief in their fellow-men. They sometimes even lose belief in their fellow-women, but I am glad to say I haven't sunk so low as that yet, for I believe in you. I do indeed," said Jack, with a sudden look of something that was not altogether jesting in his eyes. "If anybody said you were not—what I think you are, I'd like to fight him."

"I am sure you believe in a great many things," said Rita quickly. (His last words had made the colour come to her face, and she was rather ashamed that it should have come.) "You pretend that you don't,—but then you are always pretending,—and it seems to me such a pity," she added gently.

"Well, I'll never do it again!" declared Jack precipitately.

But this was a rash promise—more easily given than kept; and of course Mr. Dallas had broken it before twenty-four more hours were past.

CHAPTER III.

THERE was a piano in the library, and Jack used to get Rita to sit before it and play accompaniments for him. On the first day on which she had heard him sing, he had played his own accompaniments, but he very soon began to decline to do this, saying that his hands were too little at home upon the instrument. So then after that she played for him, and Jack liked this arrangement. Presently too, at his request, she began to sing with him,—and he liked this still more.

He told her that their voices went remarkably well together. She said that she did not perceive it (and in fact, though he sang with spirit, his intonation was by no means quite correct), but he declared that the fault was in her perception, for the fact was as he said. So they ceased to argue the question, but they did not cease to sing together. Mr. Dallas had not practised his music so assiduously for many a year as he did during these weeks.

He had a pleasant voice, Rita thought, and perhaps as the days went on she got to be pretty tolerant of the faults in his execution. She liked well enough to play for him.

"I am afraid I bother you dreadfully," he said to her sometimes, "but you see it's a rare thing for me to get a chance like this,—and I'm so desperately out of practice. When I am in London I have nobody to play for me,—not a sister, nor even a cousin. In fact, I think, without these relations it's a mistake in a man to sing at all, for he can't be always drawing on the kindness of his chance acquaintance. Water can't be expected to be as thick as blood, you know."

"And have you really no relations at all?" Rita asked compassionately one day, and then he amused himself by telling a little of his family history to her.

"I've got a sister," he said, "but if she were to come here to-morrow, I don't believe I should know her from Eve. I haven't seen her for these twenty years, and I don't suppose I shall ever see her again. She wasn't a bad girl when I knew her,—but unluckily she married, and her husband took her to New Zealand,—and there she is now, with about a dozen children hanging round her. She was my only sister,—but she's lost to me altogether, you perceive. And I had an elder brother, and he got drowned at sea."

" Oh, dear!" cried Rita pityingly.

" Yes—he was rather a fine fellow," said Jack indifferently. " He was a sailor, and he lost his life in saving somebody else who fell overboard. The man who tumbled over was picked up, thanks to Dick, and wasn't a bit the worse for his ducking, but poor Dick got struck on the head somehow—and they dragged him back on deck, but it was all over with him then. Queer that a promising young life like that should be snuffed out in such a way—wasn't it?" asked Mr. Dallas, without any touch of sentiment in his voice.

" Was he older than you?" inquired Rita after a few moments.

" Oh, dear me, yes," said Jack. " Ten
71

years older. I was quite a little chap when he died. He used to give me sugar-plums, and bring me outlandish toys from foreign places. And he used to box my ears too. I had rather an objection to that, for he had a particularly heavy hand,—but little boys have to bear a great deal, so I suffered in silence. I think, however, that when he was gone the reflection that I should never be cuffed again mitigated my sorrow a good deal. You never had your ears boxed, Miss Rita. If you had, you would have sympathized with my feelings."

"Your father and mother must have been very proud of him," said Rita, after another little silence. (She wisely treated Jack's last remarks with the contempt they deserved, and made no response of any kind to them.)

"Well,—yes," replied Mr. Dallas thoughtfully. "I suppose they were. It's a weakness, of course, to admire a man so much who throws his life away, but we all indulge in it. I have even had some thought myself, at moments when I've been sick of the world, of becoming a hero, and making a decent ending that way; but, you see, the difficulty is that it's not a kind of thing you can take to in cold blood. That consideration has always deterred me. And now, I begin to suspect, I'm getting too old for it; for, if you will inquire into the matter, Miss Rita, you will find that the heroic is a line of life that men don't much take up after they have lost their youth. They can continue it beyond that time, but they seldom start it, I should say, after they've turned five-and-thirty. That's unlucky for me, you see! But I never had much luck —somehow. I wasn't born with a silver

spoon in my mouth as your father was.
Come and let us sing a song. I can't even
sing well: upon my word, I don't think
there's anything I do well in this world!
And I've lost even the chance of dying the
death of a hero. Ah, well!" said Jack, and
rose from his seat with a sigh that found a
sympathetic echo in Rita's kind young
breast.

For he often made the girl sorry—she
hardly knew why. He seemed so light-
hearted on the surface, and yet beneath the
surface she thought that he was sometimes so sad. "Papa, why did Mr. Dallas
never marry? Did he never *want* to marry
anybody?" she had asked her father before
this.

At this present time she looked on him
as past the age at which he could provide
himself with a wife, but long ago, surely

74

there must have been somebody that he had cared for? Godfrey, however, could tell her nothing.

"I never heard any story about him," he said, "and he never refers to anything. I don't imagine that there has been much romance in his life. All people don't fall in love, Rita. Did you suppose they did?"

And then Rita blushed a little, and said she did not know.

"I must really go after the new year," Jack said one day. "If I stay till the 4th I shall have been here for three weeks. Now three weeks is an unconscionable length for a visit."

"If you go on the 4th, we shall expect you back at Easter," Godfrey said. "You may as well make up your mind to come at Easter. It is not till April, and the country will be looking well then."

"But you won't want me," said Jack—
"will you? If I come again so soon as
that, I don't know what Rita would say."

Though he made this speech, however,
perhaps he did know pretty well what
Rita would say.

"Oh," exclaimed the girl quickly, "you
know I should like it."

She spoke very cordially—possibly unconscious that as she did it her heart began to
beat quicker than usual. She was only
anxious to make him sure that he should
be welcome if he came again. But something in her few words touched Jack
enough to make him silent.

"Well, you are an enviable fellow," he
said that day to Godfrey. "I think, do
you know, that I could take to a daughter
pretty kindly, if I had one. Daughters
are institutions something like sunshine,

it seems to me. At least that is the conclusion Rita has made me come to—bless
her. I believe I shall want to come back
at Easter just to see her again."

Mr. Dallas had been improving a little
in his horsemanship during the weeks that
he had been at Ivor; but he was de-
veloping, both Godfrey and Rita thought,
rather into a rash rider than a steady one.
They had mounted him at first upon a
very quiet animal, but as his confidence
increased so did his ambition, and before
he reached the end of his visit he had
persuaded Godfrey to allow him to try a
horse of greater spirit.

"You might let me have Jessie," he
told him. "I believe I could get on with
Jessie capitally. This old Killigrew has
really no more go in him than a donkey."

"He is very safe," Godfrey suggested.

"Well, so would the donkey be," exclaimed Jack. "But nevertheless you wouldn't like to ride it."

And then Godfrey laughed, and said he was quite welcome to have Jessie if he thought he could manage her; and Mr. Dallas had Jessie accordingly, and after his first trial professed himself perfectly satisfied with her.

"She's a splendid horse," he said. "It's wonderful how much better one rides with an animal like this under one."

"Yes, she's a very good horse," Godfrey answered; "but you will find that she needs a little humouring."

"Oh, I'll humour her," answered Jack; and (he was still on her back) as he spoke he playfully touched her with his whip, upon which she bolted forward, and Jack had some little ado to keep his seat.

"Now, what in the world made her do that?" he inquired of Godfrey curiously, when he had regained his control of her. "I merely gave her the slightest possible whisk." And to illustrate his former proceeding he raised his whip again. But before he could bring it down Godfrey arrested his arm.

"I wouldn't do that a second time if I were you," he said drily. "Jessie doesn't like having her ears flicked. If you don't take the hint she has given you, the chances are she will make it broader next time."

"Oh, I think I could stick on, even if she did," replied Jack with rash confidence. But still for the moment he wisely followed his friend's advice, and for the rest of his ride left the mare's ears alone.

The day that followed this one was to

be the last of his stay with them. It was rather an ungenial morning, but Godfrey had business which obliged him to go out, and Jack, on the plea that he would not have another chance, urged that Rita and he should take their horses and accompany him. "We can leave you when you get to Merton, and come back by ourselves," he said. So they agreed to this, and started—Mr. Dallas on Jessie's back again—and at the end of an hour Rita and Jack left Godfrey at his destination, and turned their faces homewards.

It was a cold morning, and the ground was crisp and the trees were white with hoar-frost. Jack was in high spirits. The sting in the air exhilarated him, he said.

"I really begin to think I could take to a country life," he exclaimed as they rode along. "I never remember to have had much of a fancy for it before ; but as one gets up in years I suppose the charms of idleness grow upon one,—and you are all so delightfully idle here. You don't know it, Miss Rita, but you are. What do you do all day but pass from one mild entertainment to another ? You ride, and you sing, and you play; you read novels, and drink tea, and talk gossip—"

" When have you heard us talk gossip ? " interrupted Rita a little indignantly.

" I haven't heard you," replied Jack unblushingly, " but I know you do it, all the same. It's in the nature of things that you should. How else could you occupy your minds ? I don't say you talk scandal—you are too kind to do that—but of course you gossip; in the country everybody does, and, as I say, it's very delightful. I begin to feel that I could get to feel a great interest in my neighbours if I had only one or two of them to the square mile. It is always the rarity of a thing that determines its value, and it gives a pleasant excitement to the mind, when you see a distant figure on the horizon, to be able to speculate as to whether he is Tom, or Dick, or Harry, with a perfect certainty that when he comes nearer you will find he is one of the three. I begin to like that. It feels friendly; it takes away all sense of isolation."

"But yet you think it stupid, all the same, I suppose," said Rita, not quite liking this jesting. "I know that in your heart you think that living in the country is *very* stupid; it amuses you for a little perhaps, as any new thing might, but that is all. You pretend sometimes to think that papa is very much to be envied, but you wouldn't live papa's life; you wouldn't bear three months of it. You would tire of everything, I believe, that was quiet and—dull."

"Ah, no doubt, if I was conscious that it was dull. Who wouldn't?" asked Jack cheerily. "Dullness is not a thing that it is natural to any human being to like. But the question is whether, if I lived here, I *should* be dull, Miss Rita, and upon my word I am getting curiously disposed to think that I shouldn't. *Pretend* to envy your father! Bless my soul, do you mean to say you doubt that I envy him? I declare I never look at him but I break the tenth commandment."

"Why? Because he is richer than you?" asked Rita severely.

And then Jack paused for a moment, and after that little pause replied with a laugh: "Yes, because he is richer than I am. There are different kinds of riches in the world, you know, and I envy him some of his most unquestionably. If I had married twenty years ago perhaps I shouldn't, but you see I didn't do that, unfortunately."

"And so now you have nobody belonging to you, you mean?" said Rita gravely. "Yes, I should think you would have been happier if you had married."

"I might have been, but it's a chance," replied Jack lightly. "As I was saying to your father the other day, it would have been awkward if, instead of having his luck, I had found myself overwhelmed with half a dozen boys. I dare say it's best as it is. The risk would have been too great. I don't like boys, Miss Rita."

"Don't you?" said Rita innocently. "Oh, I do. I mean, when they're nice."

" But they're never nice," exclaimed Jack. " Some are a trifle better than others; that is about all you can say for them. I read this morning in the paper of one who robbed his father of £78—all the savings he had in the world. That is the sort of thing they do, you see. You never heard of a girl robbing her father of £78? No; if I had married I should have liked to have one daughter. No boys, and just one girl; neither more nor less. But, as I repeat, the risk was too great, so I never ran it, and here I am, at forty-four, without a tie in the world, or a soul who would miss me if my life got ended to-morrow. That is cheering, isn't it?"

" No, it is not cheering, and it is not true," said Rita. " It is not true," she repeated quickly, but half shyly, " for we should miss you here."

"Would you, do you think?" asked Jack. "Well, that is kindly said, at any rate. And if I happened to get knocked on the head just at this moment, for instance, I do believe you would be sorry. So that's something. And as for the rest, there are worse things in the world than to be forced to live alone in it, though perhaps I may not take kindly to my solitude again all at once when I get back to it to-morrow. Just imagine the contrast! Picture me to yourself as I shall be—say, when I come down to breakfast on Friday morning—the room filled with a London fog, my chimney probably smoking, my coffee cold, my eggs too stale to eat. The eggs are always stale in town, you know. I don't understand how they manage it."

"You shall take some fresh ones back with you," said Rita. "You sha'n't have them stale for a few mornings at any rate. I don't think I should like to live in London!"

"Of course you wouldn't," exclaimed Jack. "It's an awful place. It only suits hardened people like me. We learn to eat olives there,—and caviare; we sleep till midday, and sit up all night. You may well wonder how we stand such a life at all, but custom does so much. We get so depraved that we even fancy sometimes that we like it."

"I dare say you will be glad to get back to it," Rita said, with a little tone of petulance in her voice. It would have pleased her if he had been sorry to go back, but he was not sorry in the least, she was afraid; he liked his town habits better than he liked theirs.

"Well, there is always a certain pleasure

when you have been out of town in finding yourself in it again," he allowed. "It is a mixed pleasure often, but it is one, more or less. Yes, in some ways I shall not be sorry to get back to it. The fish is at home in his native element, you know, —and work can't be done in Paradise."

"But this is not Paradise," Rita said.

And then Jack laughed, and asked her how she knew that. "There are many kinds of Paradises," he told her, "and I have come to the conclusion not only that this is one of them, but that it is about the best one that I'm just now acquainted with. I've been amazingly happy in it, at any rate, and I ought morally to be amazingly the better for it too, though whether I *shall* be—"

Mr. Dallas had just reached this point, and was pausing a moment before he finished his sentence, when his evil genius prompted him most gratuitously to apply his whip again, as he had already done upon the previous day, to Jessie's ears—an almost unconscious movement that, however, had disastrous results, for the mare, resenting it, rose suddenly on her hind legs, and then immediately afterwards plunged forwards, and sent Jack (too much amazed almost to make an effort to keep his seat) clean over her head upon the ground. He got his feet out of the stirrups happily, but he performed a complete summersault, and fell flat on the hard road upon his back, while Jessie galloped on with her reins flying loose, and Rita gave a scream of alarm that Jack heard remorsefully even in the midst of his own consternation.

The whole thing happened in little more than a second or two.

"Oh, I'm all right!" Mr. Dallas gasped almost instantly, and tried to raise himself; but he could not raise himself, and sank back with a groan.

And then Rita jumped down, and came to his side, with all the colour gone from her face.

"Are you hurt? Oh, I am afraid you are hurt! Oh, what shall I do?" she exclaimed, gazing at him in distress. "Do you think if you took my hand—?" And she held out both hands.

But though he took them, and made another effort to lift himself up with the help of them, he failed again; and then, as she felt his quivering convulsive grasp, poor little soul, her face puckered up, and she began to cry with distress and fright.

Jack had been confounded enough

already, but this sight fairly overwhelmed him.

"My dear, don't do that," he exclaimed panting. "It's—it's nothing probably. Get on your horse again, and go away. Look here—I'll just stay as I am till you can send somebody. I've been an awful fool, but, you'll make an end of me altogether if you cry over me."

· "But I can't bear to leave you," said Rita almost sobbing.

"Well, you see, you can't do any-thing else," replied Jack with much com-mon sense; "for I can't move, and it's clear you can't get me home without some help."

And then he set his teeth, for he was in enough pain to make it hard work for him to keep from groaning, and closed his eyes; and poor Rita with a terrible dread of what might happen before she could bring any assistance to him, got on her horse again, and galloped home as fast as she could go, with her face as white as a sheet.

CHAPTER IV.

A couple of hours after this Mr. Dallas
was lying in bed, under strict injunctions
to keep upon his back, and not unneces-
arily to move a limb. He was not in any
danger of dying, Dr. Carson said, but he
had given himself an ugly wrench, and
must make up his mind to be some weeks
before he got over it.

"But—God bless me!—I must get back
to town! I've got work to do," he cried
at this announcement.

"I dare say you have," Dr. Carson
replied. "It is what most of us have got.

But unless there should be any of it that you can do here presently, it will have to remain undone. You should have thought of your work before you began to play tricks with your mare's ears."

" I wish to heaven I had ! " groaned Jack.

He had already made the most contrite and self-reproachful declarations to Godfrey.

" I don't know what devil of ill luck possessed me ! " he had ejaculated. " I never was so ashamed of myself in my life. I was merely talking, and, by way of emphasizing my words, I suppose I must have—have given her a little cut on her head. It was the most foolish thing to do, but it only proves what a fool I am altogether, and how I ought never to have been on a horse's back at all. Now I am going to be a pretty burden on you ! "

But Godfrey, as may be supposed, took that part of the matter very lightly.

"You will be no burden to anybody here," he said. "You will only be an interest. All the neighbourhood will watch your case."

"And will set me down for an idiot," exclaimed Jack. "Ah, that's cheerful! The next time I act like a fool I only hope I may do it in the midst of the safe solitude of London." And he turned his face away, almost in earnest in his last words, for without any jesting he felt humiliated.

"There is little Rita, too : even *she* will be laughing at me presently," he thought, "when she has got over her fright. I *did* frighten her, poor little maid ! What a face she had !"—and it troubled him to recall it. He was not a man who suffered much from vanity, but he must have made himself ridiculous in her sight, he reflected, and, to tell the truth, he was sorry for it.

"I wonder when I shall see her again; I should like to see her—just to say a word or two," he began to think.

At present, however, he was not likely to see her, for Dr. Carson ordered him to keep his bed, and, naturally, Rita was not amongst the nurses appointed to attend to him there.

It was Godfrey and Mrs. Helstone and Miss Taylor who undertook to look after him, and they all of them spent so much time in his room, and tried with so much assiduity to lighten the tedium of his confinement, that Rita, left pretty much alone, and allowed to take no part in the labour that employed the others, felt the days hang rather heavily on her hands. It was stupid to have no part in what the rest were doing, she thought ; it was stupid, and it made her dull.

"I wish Mr. Dallas would get well," she said rather dolefully to her father when Jack had been four days in bed ; but at this Godfrey shook his head.

"He is not likely to get well yet," he replied. "You must have patience, my dear. If he is able to be about by the end of three weeks you may be content."

"But he won't have to stay in *bed* for three weeks—will he ?" exclaimed Rita. "Oh, I hope he won't, for it is so dreadfully lonely ! "

And then Godfrey laughed. He knew that his daughter was not fond of solitude.

"Poor little deserted woman !" he said. "But have patience ; Mr. Dallas will be allowed a change of position, I hope, before long."

And, indeed, a few days afterwards, to Rita's delight, Dr. Carson gave his patient permission to get upon a couch, and be wheeled from his room into another on the same floor, which had been hastily converted into a temporary sitting-room for him, Rita making it pretty with books and flowers and ornaments.

She took this work upon herself, and was delighted with her occupation.

"My dear, you need not do so much," her grandmother said to her, looking in once on her operations, and finding her busily decorating the mantel-piece with pictures and vases and fans; but Rita turned round at this speech with a disappointed face.

"Oh, but I want to make it nice," she said.

"Well, child, it *is* nice," replied Mrs.

Helstone. "It is quite as nice as it need be. A man, you know, doesn't care for the little prettinesses that please a girl. Mr. Dallas won't notice your pots and vases, Rita."

"No—he won't notice them, perhaps, but if they were away he might think the place looked bare, it seemed to me," said Rita gently. She surveyed her unfinished work with a little sigh. "I should like to go on doing it as I had meant," she said pleadingly. "You see, we shall all be here."

And then, of course, Mrs. Helstone gave in, and, with renewed spirit, Rita resumed her labours. Very likely Mr. Dallas would not notice anything. Her grandmother might be quite right in that, but nevertheless she liked to think that she was adorning the room for him.

She had been so sorry about his accident, and all the others had been able since it happened to do so much for him, and she had never been able to do anything—until now. It seemed to her such a long time since that day when he had frightened her so. She wondered a little if he knew how very sorry she had been for him. As the time came near to-day for her to see him again, she felt rather shy at the prospect of their meeting. She did not quite know what she ought to say to him; it was always difficult, she thought, to know what to say to people who had been ill. She could not make up her mind at all as to the sort of greeting it would be right to give him: she could not even tell whether he would expect her to be grave or not. He seldom seemed to expect anybody to be grave, she reflected, but yet this occasion

100

was different from any ordinary one, and perhaps he might like to take it seriously. As she dressed her chimney-piece she went on thinking the matter over, again and again. It was not worth thinking so much about, but while her hands were busy she had nothing better to do.

She was waiting in the room, when early in the afternoon they wheeled Jack in. He entered head foremost, lying on his back, with abundant wraps about him, for the weather was cold; and he also entered talking.

"The most natural thing perhaps would be to come in the other way," she heard him announcing, "but the other way is the fashion at funerals, so it seems cheerier to have it like this. Bless me, what a nice little room!—and—upon my word—there's Rita! Oh, Rita, I've thought of you a great many times." And then he dis-engaged a hand from his rugs, and put it out to her with a little twitch about his lips that he tried to hide.

She went forward and took his hand, but to her vexation she found she could not say a word. It was very stupid, but she felt suddenly that all the various little greetings she had rehearsed beforehand had vanished one and all from her mind. She shook hands with him,—and that was the whole. And then, almost in another moment he had begun to talk again.

"Not with my head quite so close to the fire," he exclaimed. "Yes—a little bit more round this way. That's it now—that's the very thing. I think this room is delightful!"

"Well, it does not make a bad sitting-room certainly," Godfrey assented. "It was a bed-room, you know. They merely took away the bed, and put in a few tables and chairs, and Rita has been at work, as you see, dressing it up a little."

"Dressing it up for me—has she? Bless her! It's more than I deserve," said Jack. "But everybody does more for me than I deserve, so it's no use to talk of it. Miss Rita, if I could, I would put dust and ashes on my head, but I can't get anybody to hand the ashes to me, and I'm so horribly, so utterly, so absurdly helpless, that I can't get them for myself. I contemplate kneeling down at your feet presently, and begging your forgiveness; but you see as yet I can't perform even that act of humility."

"I wish you wouldn't talk so! I don't think you ought," said Rita colouring, and speaking for the first time, and then Jack looked at her with a smile and told her heartily that he liked to hear her scolding him again.

"For I haven't had anybody to scold me all this week," he said, "and I have felt as if my moral nature had not been properly looked after. But you always look after it, you know, and pull me up when I go wrong, and I think that system agrees with me. I believe I must have a natural leaning towards virtue, for being with you always seems to suit me so. It does indeed. Now, if you would sit down there—Oh," breaking off abruptly, "what's this? Gruel?"

"Gruel? No:" said Mrs. Helstone. "Gruel at this time of day! It's your soup. Didn't you say you would take it as soon as you came in here?"

"Ah, I believe I did. You're quite

right,—and excellent soup it looks," exclaimed Jack cheerily.

And then Godfrey prepared to raise him up, and Mrs. Helstone began to arrange his pillows, and Rita, fearing that they might not wish her to stay during these operations, slipped silently out of the room.

She would rather have liked to stay, only she was shy of staying, so she went down-stairs reluctantly, and spent an hour by herself; and then at the end of that time her father called her back and told her that Mr. Dallas wanted to see her again.

"He would like you to sit with him for a little," he said. "I am going out, and grandmamma is going home."

So Rita willingly returned to Jack's little parlour, and was welcomed very cordially.

"Am I very rude to send for you?"

he asked as she came in. "I am afraid
I am, but, you see, everybody is giving
me my own way just now, and it seems
to be generally understood that I am to
have a royal time of it. The princes of
the blood (as I have been told, for I don't
associate with them myself), when they
want to talk to a lady, send for her, and
so, following their example, I've ventured
to send for you, for you ran away so
unexpectedly a little while ago. Why in
the world did you run away? I had hardly
spoken a word to you."

"But you were going to have your
dinner," explained Rita.

"Well, people can have their dinner and
talk too—can't they?" said Jack. "Indeed
you always *ought* to talk when you dine,
as every doctor will tell you,—and you
forget that I haven't seen you all the

week. Oh, my dear, I've been bothered about you!—and I've been awfully ashamed of myself—that's a fact."

"But you shouldn't be ashamed. I hope you are not saying that seriously?" exclaimed Rita with earnestness.

"It has been as much as I could do, lying in my bed over there, to keep from swearing," said Jack. "I knew that if I swore I should make it worse for myself, so I didn't do it, but it was a hard matter to keep my tongue quiet, I can tell you, whenever I thought of that poor little face of yours. You don't know what a frightened face it was when I saw it last. The memory of it has been lying on my conscience like a lump of lead."

"It was so stupid of me," said Rita deprecatingly. "I never am brave when I ought to be. I always cry when I am frightened, and it makes me so vexed afterwards. I am *very* sorry that I cried that day, for I know it made you uncomfortable."

"Ah, I suppose I told you so—didn't I?" asked Jack instantly. "I've no doubt I did: it would be just like me,—always thinking of myself and not of anybody else. Well, I made a pretty mess of it! I should like to know what you have been thinking of me ever since? It wouldn't be pleasant to hear, but it would be salutary, I've no doubt,—so suppose you tell me as a matter of discipline. Come now— begin."

But Rita was looking at him with a puzzled face.

"I don't know what you mean," she said.

"I mean that I want you to scoff at me, and have done with it," he answered. "I don't like things to be hanging over my head,—and this has been hanging over me for the last eight days."

" *What* has ? " she said. " You are talking very oddly; I wish you wouldn't. How could I scoff at you when I have only been so very sorry ? "

" But you know I made a fool of myself ? "

" I—didn't think so."

" I did what nobody but an ass would have done—meddling with that beast's ears again. Upon my life I can't tell how I did it. I was thinking no more of the creature than you were."

" No; but that was just it, I suppose."

" Because I ought to have been thinking, you mean ? Well, yes, of course I ought. A man is an idiot who rides an animal and forgets her idiosyncrasies. That's one of the bores of being on horseback. I think it is quite enough when I'm out to take care of myself, without needing to take care of a mare as well. But I say again, I was a fool, and you must have thought so.— Did you not?" after a moment's silence.

"I am sure"—shyly—"you must know I didn't."

"I should like to believe you, but I hardly can. Do you know it nearly made me blush when I saw you an hour ago. I said to myself, 'There she is, and if she spoke what she thought she would call out, "You old fool!"' And then, when you made off as soon as ever you had shaken hands with me—"

"Oh, how can you talk such nonsense!" she exclaimed. "Mr. Dallas, I wish you wouldn't."

"But you did make off, you know, and

you wouldn't have come back if I hadn't sent for you."

"Oh yes, I should. I was only wait-ing—because I didn't know—" And then she stopped.

"Because you didn't know what? Whether I wanted you? My dear, I always want you in this house, it seems to me. You are such a natural part of it that when you are absent I feel some-thing missing. Now take this moment, for instance,—I wasn't at ease before you came, because I thought you would sneer at me; but you don't seem to be sneer-ing, so I find your presence very com-fortable. Do you know, I shall have to be here for another fortnight?"

"Yes, and I am very glad," said Rita.

"Glad!" interrupted Jack; "I don't want you to be glad. If I had said I expected to be upon my feet to-morrow, and you had expressed some satisfaction at *that* intelligence—"

"Oh, but you don't understand! Of course I am sorry that you can't get up," said Rita.

"Then if you are sorry why do you say you are glad? You shouldn't say one thing and mean another; it isn't right, you know."

"But you *will* misunderstand," reiterated Rita.

"I don't see that I misunderstand. When I told you I should have to lie here for another fortnight I expected you to say something sympathetic. It looks like malice for you to exclaim at once that you are glad."

"Oh, Mr. Dallas!" cried the girl.

And then he looked up at her, and
112

something in her face made him suddenly repent, and put out his hand to her, and begin to laugh.

"Why, you don't mean that you mind my talking so?" he exclaimed. "Surely you know I am only joking?"

"I *didn't* know," answered Rita, with a momentary quiver in her voice. "It is always so difficult to know whether you are serious, or only making fun. But I think you are almost never serious," she added in a condemnatory tone. "It is very foolish of me ever to be taken in by you."

"It would be odd, though, if you weren't," responded Mr. Dallas, half below his breath.

"*What* would be odd?" asked Rita, putting her head forward. But Jack thought it wisest not to repeat his remark.

"I was only moralizing: I have a great habit of moralizing aloud," he explained. "It's a very bad habit, so I wouldn't advise you to fall into it. Anything like a peculiarity, Miss Rita, is a thing to be avoided. In your course through life remember that. Unfortunately, *I* have a great many peculiarities."

"Have you?" asked Rita. "Then—why don't you try to get rid of them?"

"Get rid of them at my age?" replied Jack, with an accent of astonishment. "Now that's absurd! Did you ever hear of anybody beginning to shake off their peculiarities with one foot in the grave?"

"I am sure you don't think you have one foot in the grave," said Rita with increasing severity. "You don't think yourself old. If you wanted to get rid of — anything, you could do it quite easily."

He lay for a moment or two placidly looking at her: then—"You are sixteen, are you not?" he said.

"Sixteen!" exclaimed Rita bridling. "I shall be eighteen in June."

"Ah, you're young for that," replied Jack reflectively. "*Very* young. I don't know how you can be so much. It is only in the earliest period of youth generally that we think we can do everything. Eighteen! Bless my heart!"

"You are trying to make me angry, but you are not going to do it," said Rita resolutely. "No, you are not," she repeated, colouring a little, and looking rather defiant.

"I know you have much ado to keep your temper, though," said Jack, with something like a chuckle. "It's odd what hot tempers we have at six— I mean, under twenty. Now *I* couldn't lose my temper over a trifle like this though I tried. I couldn't, I protest! I've lost the power of being peppery. Youth is a very imperfect thing, Miss Rita. You will be a vast deal improved, you will find, when you have got quit of it, and are ten or twelve years older. That will be a long time after this, and I shall hardly live, I am afraid, to see it; but when it comes you must think of me, and of what I am telling you now. It is my belief that at thirty you will be a very nice, composed, sensible woman."

"I wonder if you have been talking— in this kind of way all these last days? Or do you only talk so to me, because you think I am so—foolish?" said Rita, bringing out the last word a little pathetically.

"*Are* you foolish?" inquired Jack calmly. And then he laughed. "Would you mind taking the trouble to hand me that book?" he asked next moment abruptly. "This is a very wise grave book that I have been trying to improve myself by reading. I got it from your father, and I think there are some things in it that would be very wholesome for you. Look here now; here is a passage I should like you to read and digest carefully."

But just as he was about to point it out to her a servant opened the door, and said that there was a visitor below who wanted to see Miss Helstone.

"Ah, and so you must go?" exclaimed Jack. "Well, that is a pity, for what I· was going to show you would have done

117

you a great deal of good. You couldn't send down word that you were taking a lesson, I suppose,—could you?"

"No, I don't think I could," replied Rita laughing.

"Oh, well then, it can't be helped," said Mr. Dallas resignedly. "But leave the book with me. I'll try and adapt the lesson to myself."

So he composed himself to read, and she went away.

"I wish he wasn't quite so odd," she thought. But yet, in spite of his oddness, she liked him well enough to be glad to go back to him, and let him talk to her again, when the visitor to whom she had been called had taken her leave.

CHAPTER V.

Mr. Dallas did not suffer much, but the doctor's orders that he should not move from his recumbent position were peremptory, so day followed day without his making much apparent advance.

"I wonder if Carson knows what he is about?" he said at last one morning speculatively to Godfrey. "Don't you think he might bring in somebody else, and have a consultation over me? It would be an awful bore, and an expense, and all that, but you don't know how it bothers me to lie here in this way like a log."

"I suspect that you are getting on as

fast as is possible," answered Godfrey, " but there is no reason why you shouldn't have a consultation if you would like it."

So he spoke to Dr. Carson, and a surgeon of reputation was sent for, who examined Jack thoroughly, but ended by agreeing entirely with the opinion of the case that Dr. Carson had already formed. Rest was all that Mr. Dallas needed, he said. There was no cause for anxiety, but he must be content for the present to remain upon his back.

" But couldn't I get up to town ?" asked Jack.

"Such a journey would be very undesirable," said the surgeon ; and then Godfrey laughed.

" He is an impatient fellow," he said. " Nobody wants him in town. He has no more need to be there than I have."

"Then," replied the surgeon, "I would decidedly advise him to stay where he is."

"And so I am expected to submit and hold my tongue, I suppose?" said Jack after this. "Well, I am helpless, and you must bear the burden of me. I'm very sorry for you all. I'm so sorry that I don't know how to speak about it."

"If that is the case," returned Godfrey, "I hope you will hold your tongue."

Mr. Dallas passed his days mainly in the little sitting-room that had been prepared for him, but his hours there were not very solitary ones, for some of the household nearly always bore him company. His most frequent attendants, either together or separately, were Godfrey and Rita. These two spent half the day in reading or talking to him. After a time he fell into the habit, on the pretext of its being

an excellent exercise, of making Rita read
to him a good deal.

"To be able to read aloud without
fatigue is a proof of good lungs and a fine
constitution," he would assure her. "At
your age you don't value these things as
you ought. You think it is interesting
to be delicate, but it isn't interesting—not
a bit. Take care of your health, and keep
your bloom. You won't be worth half
what you are at present if you don't. So,
to help you to expand your chest a little
more, suppose you give me another
chapter."

And then she would laugh probably,
but she would also do what he told
her.

There are few tasks more pleasant to the
majority of women than to minister to
some one they like, who is helpless, and

Rita's taste for this sort of work became developed very rapidly during the weeks while Jack lay on his back. She was so very sorry for him that of course she liked to do what she could to relieve the tedium of his days. "It must be so dreadfully dull for you," she would say to him pityingly.

"When a woman is ill it doesn't seem half so sad," she said once. "You see, we can do things to amuse ourselves that you can't. We can knit—and sew."

"And do you mean to say it amuses you to knit and sew?" exclaimed Jack. "Bless my heart, it wouldn't amuse me! Why should any one ever want to knit as long as there are books in the world, or people to be talked to?"

"Oh, one likes it for a change," said Rita. But Mr. Dallas shook his head.

"I can't endure changes," he declared. "I hate and abominate them. I've known nothing but changes all my life, and what I want now is to get hold of something I care for, and keep it for ever."

"But that's impossible," said Rita.

"What of that?" returned Jack. "Is it not allowable to long for impossible things? Miss Rita, I am afraid your nature wants imagination. When I was your age (it is a long time ago, but I *was* your age once) my imagination was so ardent that it was capable of soaring to any height. I thought I could climb Parnassus then, and take my seat on the highest spur of it. Odd, wasn't it? seeing that in reality I've never gone a yard up the mountain at all. But I only mention the fact to show you the fallacy of urging the impossibility of a thing as a reason

124

for not entertaining the thought of it. It gave me a vast deal of pleasure to think of climbing Parnassus. The actual getting up, if I had ever attempted it, wouldn't have been half so delightful—or probably either half so innocent. For, just consider, I might have met somebody else going up too, and have tried to take an unfair advantage of him,—jostled him on one side, or even tripped him over a precipice perhaps. And then think what an awful burden on my soul that would have been for ever after!"

"Yes; but as if you were likely to have done that!" exclaimed Rita scornfully.

And then Mr. Dallas gave his head another shrewd and mournful shake.

"It would have been the likeliest thing in the world," he said. "Do you think, even as it is, that I have never given a

push to anybody?—not a big thrust, perhaps, but just a little sly jog with my
elbow that did him a mischief?"

"No; I don't think you ever have,"
answered Rita quickly.

The colour had come into her face, and
something in her look and in her tone
touched Jack, and made him suddenly
silent. He held his peace for about the
space of ten seconds, and when he spoke
again after that his remark was made in
a low voice, as if he were merely addressing
it to himself.

"Well, it's a good deal to have somebody
believe in one! I'll make a note of that,"
he said.

"You will—make a note of it!" echoed
Rita, rather alarmed.

"Yes, for future reference and en-
couragement," explained Jack.

"You shouldn't laugh at me," said the girl a little plaintively.

"My dear!" ejaculated Jack quickly, and with sudden energy he almost raised himself from his pillow,—"Laugh at you! May I never see your face again if I was laughing!"

"I thought you were," said Rita timidly.

"I never was further from it in my life— never! Just see what it is not to have an expressive face and voice! Miss Rita," said Jack suddenly, "if I have made myself misunderstood, let me speak again gravely, and say—thank you. I am grateful to you if you think well of me. I should be more humbled than I can tell you if I found you thought very badly of me."

"Oh, you mustn't speak so," cried Rita, blushing with confusion. "As if it could matter—"

127

"Well, seeing that you are the daughter of one of my oldest friends," said Jack, "I consider that it may very naturally matter."

And then Rita murmured something rather inarticulately, and turned away with her cheeks on fire. She did not know why she was blushing, and why her heart was beating quickly; she only knew that Mr. Dallas somehow had upset her, and that she was—well, not angry, nor sorry, nor perhaps glad, but yet unexpectedly and unreasonably touched.

She had to go out to the village presently, and as she took her walk she recalled some of the words that he had spoken with an almost frightened surprise. "I should feel more humbled than I could tell you if I found that you thought very badly of me," was what he had said,—a sentence that began to ring in her ears,—that she

could not dismiss again from her memory.
Humbled if *she* thought badly of him! She
was little more than a child, and he a
man as old as her father, but yet she knew
he had said this gravely, and a curious
feeling of gratitude to him began to stir
in her heart because of it. She felt raised
by it in her own eyes, and made more of
a woman,—made, somehow, to stand more
on a level with him, as if he had stretched
out a hand and drawn her near. And,
though she did not reason about it, the
feeling of this was pleasant to Rita, for
she was at the age when youth, to the
possessor of it, seems rather an undesirable
thing, and those earn most regard who
seem most to forget it. This period is a
fleeting one, but at least it comes for a short
time to most people, and Rita just now was
in the midst of it, and so, as it chanced,

peculiarly likely to be touched by the assertion that Mr. Dallas had made.

"Humbled if *I* thought ill of him!" she went on repeating to herself again and again, with a timid, half-complacent wonder. And he meant it too; he was quite in earnest; she was convinced of that. "If he had said it in fun I should have hated him!" she exclaimed once impetuously; but the pleasant part of the matter was that she was so sure he had not said it in fun. He joked a great deal, but he had not been joking when he told her that. And he was more than forty years old, and yet, if she had not thought well of him he had said he should feel humbled! "I think it was—*very* nice of him; it was more than most people would have said," was the final and satisfactory conclusion that she had come to by the time her walk had ended.

But as for Mr. Dallas, perhaps the sentence that had made so much impression on Rita had merely crossed his lips and been forgotten, for when they met next in the course of another hour or two there was no increased deference in his manner to her, nor indeed any visible change in it,— a little perhaps to her disappointment. She came into his parlour while he was having his tea, and he greeted her quite in his ordinary fashion.

"At it again, you see!" he merely said cheerfully, nodding his head at her, and then he went on eating the bread and butter with which he was engaged, and chatting to Miss Taylor, who was sitting by his side,—and Rita took up her embroidery, and began to occupy herself with it.

She thought presently that he was talking a great deal of nonsense, and she gave a sigh as she thought this, and wondered why he always said so many absurd things. He was always making people laugh, and it was not, Rita reflected sagely, a very high thing to make people laugh. She was glad her father was not so fond of joking. "And it is just a bad habit, because he can be so very nice and sensible—at times," Rita thought regretfully, and sewed away, making dainty daisies on a delicate bit of cloth, and looking so engrossed in her work that presently Jack called to her, and accused her of not listening to a word he said.

"I have been talking till I am hoarse, and you won't pay the least attention," he said.

"But you have not been talking to *me*," answered Rita quickly.

"Begging your pardon," returned Mr.

Dallas, "I *was* talking to you. I was talking to whoever might chance to be in the room. Miss Taylor has kindly given me her ear so far, but I have tired her now, and she is going to leave me—"

"I am *obliged* to leave you," interrupted Miss Taylor laughing,—"and, if you would take my advice, you would lie still a little now, Mr. Dallas, and rest."

But Mr. Dallas at this suggestion vigorously shook his head.

"No, no; there would be no good in that at all," he said. "If you must go, and if Miss Rita won't talk to me, I wish somebody would look up Mr. Helstone, and send him here."

"I don't know why you should say that I won't talk to you," exclaimed Rita, rising up upon this, and flushing. "That is such nonsense! Papa is out, or else I would tell him to come. But you shouldn't say things that are not true."

" Well, then, you shouldn't make me say them," retorted Jack coolly. " You ought to try instead to amuse me. Miss Taylor has been amusing me. Miss Taylor is a very nice woman. Do you know, each day I see her I like her better and better."

" Yes, she is very nice," answered Rita. "I don't know what we should do without her now. She has been so very good to me always, and especially these last two years —from the time mamma died," said Rita suddenly, speaking with a lowered voice.

"Ah, to be sure!" cried Jack quickly, " I've often thought she must have been a comfort when you lost your mother. Poor little Rita! They're awful things—these losses. And she was—ahem!—she was so —domestic, wasn't she?"

"Mamma?" asked Rita, wondering a little. "Oh yes. Oh, she was so good. I didn't half know it at the time. That is the worst so often—isn't it?"

"Well, yes," said Jack. "It's bad when that happens, and when one has to reproach oneself,—and I'm afraid, as you say, it does happen pretty often. I've had my own experience of it, for I lost my father when I was a lad."

"Did you?" Rita came a little nearer, looking at him with interest. "How old were you?"

"I was seventeen."

"And I was sixteen. I mean when mamma died. Was your father long ill?"

"No; he died of heart disease. He never was ill at all. He had been sitting talking to us—to my mother and me—one evening, and he rose from his chair, and seemed as if he was going to cross the room, and—that was the end of it. He was gone before we could stretch out a hand to him. Poor father!—I don't know that I was ever much comfort to him, except the first time that I stood up before him and conjugated a Latin verb. He gave me half-a-crown on that occasion; and I would gladly have conjugated any number more Latin verbs for him on the same terms—but somehow he never made the offer to me again. I've thought since that it might have added to his happiness if he had."

Rita had drawn nearer to him, though with a little hesitation, during this speech. Before she replied to it she had taken possession of Miss Taylor's vacated seat.

"It would be terrible to have anybody

one loved die in that sudden way," she said half below her breath. "How dreadfully sorry you must have been!"

"Well—I suppose I was," Jack said, but he spoke a little dubiously. "I dare say I was—if a boy is ever what he ought to be. But I don't think he ever is. Oh, boys altogether are a bad lot."

"I don't believe you think that." Rita made this declaration, however, a little uneasily.

"I protest I do. I can't endure them. I would put every boy I met, if I could, under a barrel. Don't let us talk of them. Thank heaven there are none here!"

"Well, I should like to have had a brother," said Rita.

"My dear, you are much better without one. Perhaps when I was as young as you I might not have said so, but, recollect,
137

youth and the love of disturbance lasts a short time, and age and the love of peace lasts a very long time, and with age comes wisdom. It seems to me that I have to recall this fact very often to your memory, Miss Rita. You haven't much respect naturally, I am sorry to say, for grey hairs and experience."

"I don't think people always get wiser as they grow older," said the girl gravely after a moment's silence. "They ought to, of course,—and some do, but "—and then she glanced at Jack and hesitated. "But, you know," she began again,—" you know quite well—some old people are *very* foolish."

"Oh yes—one here and there," answered Jack carelessly. "But that's nothing. As a rule, maturity is full of wisdom. I beg your pardon—" looking at her suddenly;

"I don't quite understand the expression on your face?"

"I suppose you talk in this kind of way just to tease me—don't you?" said Rita rather wistfully. "I mean, when you say silly things it is not because you think them really, but you say them just to make me wonder?"

"When I say silly things!" repeated Jack, and he echoed her words so sternly that poor Rita began to blush, and made a hasty explanation.

"I mean *odd* things—the kind of things you say so often."

"You mean *wise* things," he corrected her reprovingly. "Things too wise for you to understand."

But she looked at him for a moment, and then she shook her head.

"No, they are not wise things," she

answered steadily. "I am sure they are not. They are often nonsense, and I don't believe you can really think them—because, if you are clever, you can't,—and papa says you are clever."

"Your father always had a great deal of discrimination," responded Jack with unction.

"Yes—but often—nobody would think you clever at all."

"Of course they wouldn't! I sincerely hope they wouldn't," said Jack fervently.

And then Rita opened her eyes, and he began to chuckle. Whenever he fairly succeeded in mystifying Miss Helstone, Mr. Dallas had a trick of chuckling to himself that was naturally rather exasperating. She threw an indignant glance at him now, and after a moment or two rose from her seat. He would not talk sensibly—he was

140

absurd—he liked to tease people just as if he was a child, she thought; and she would have left him in disdain if suddenly those words he had spoken in the afternoon had not come back to her mind, and touched her, and made her in charity with him again.

"He is nicer than he often seems; he was *very* nice only a few hours ago," she thought. And so she hesitated for a moment or two, and then turned her head half-round to him, and—"Shall I read something to you?" she said abruptly.

"Well, if you won't go on talking, read to me by all means," he answered. "Look —here's our book." And as he held it out, and she came to take it from him—"Kind little Rita!" he said suddenly.

"Oh, you mustn't call me kind," she exclaimed remorsefully. "I—was cross just now."

141

"Then it was my fault," he answered, "because I plagued you. But you are a forgiving little girl,—and I like forgiving people. There now—sit down in your own seat. You are not stopping with me, are you, when you have something else to do?"

"Oh no; I have nothing else to do," she said.

"Well, that's all right. Then I may make myself comfortable. It's a rare blessing for *me* that you haven't got those brothers you were talking of. Troublesome young scamps! They would be in and out here all day long, and I should never get a quiet half-hour with you. No, no; you're better as you are,—a vast deal better. Now then!"

And as Mr. Dallas composed himself to listen, Rita opened her book.

CHAPTER VI.

It occupied Rita very much to wait on Mr. Dallas, and supply him with the various forms of entertainment that he required; but then she had little else to do, so she gave her services very easily. She liked his company too apparently, in spite of the faults she found in him, for she never seemed to care to be absent from him long, and he, on his side, when she came to him made her always demonstratively welcome. Their regard for one another was like the regard of uncle and niece, Godfrey and Miss Taylor thought, not dreaming of anything deeper and stronger. But by the time he was beginning to get upon his feet again Jack at any rate probably knew that the case between him and Rita had come to be something very different from what they supposed.

His convalescence was a slow business enough. When a month had passed after his accident he was still only in a condition to walk for a few minutes at a time, and a fortnight more elapsed before he was pronounced to be even nearly fit to return home.

" Upon my word, this is trying for you !" he would often exclaim to his host.

" I would try to make my escape," he said once, " only, you see, it's so awkward to attempt to run away when you can't get down-stairs. If ever I run the risk of a thing like this again——"

"Better take some riding lessons," answered Godfrey to this speech. "That is what I would advise you to do presently. Nothing of this would have happened if you had known how to sit a horse."

But Jack shook his head. "I've had enough of horses," he said prudently. "It's little use to a man in London to know how to ride. One has to get behind the brutes even there in hansoms, but it is one thing to be behind them, where you have no responsibility, and quite another thing to be on their backs."

"Well, but you cut yourself out of a pleasure," Godfrey urged.

"I might find it a pleasure to dance on the tight-rope," retorted Jack, "but nevertheless I am not going to learn."

And then Godfrey laughed and held his peace.

The weather grew very mild in February, and in the soft early spring days Mr. Dallas began to take walks about the garden, and in these walks it rarely happened that Rita failed to accompany him. He would pace slowly up and down the gravelled paths, with a stick in one hand, and with his other hand upon her arm. "Take *my* arm," Godfrey said at first, and once or twice Mr. Dallas did so, but presently he said he found that Rita's suited him the best. "It is just the height I seem to want," he asserted, "so, if she doesn't mind——" And of course Rita did not mind; or, rather, she did mind enough to be disappointed if he accepted any other support than hers.

The girl knew vaguely by that time that in all her life she had never been so happy as she was now; she knew too that she liked Mr. Dallas very much indeed; but what their intimacy and their mutual regard meant and was to end in she had not ventured to ask herself. He was so much older than she was that perhaps it never alarmed her to find how constantly she thought about him; they were only friends, of course: how could they be anything else? It was true that she was always getting to care for being with him more and more, and that the prospect of his going away was something she could not bear to face; but friends may be very dear indeed to one, and Rita believed that she and Jack were only friends. He had been very good to her, and they had been a great deal together,—and she had got fond of him, because she did not know how anybody could help doing that, she only thought. So she lived from day to day,

147

basking in the sunshine that was round her, and happily treading the pleasant road on which her feet were set without inquiring to what bourne it was leading her.

But Mr. Dallas knew where it was leading *him*, at any rate, and these days were gradually making him more serious than his wont, and inducing many thoughts and speculations in him regarding an until now unexpected future. He was getting troubled too, feeling that something was going on which it was not right should go on without Godfrey Helstone's knowledge. His conscience had become uneasy. "I must speak to him," he thought, "and ten to one he won't like it. I shouldn't in his place, I know. I'm hanged if I should! But I'm in for it now, and there's no help but to make a clean breast of it,—and the sooner the better too."

So Jack passed a few uncomfortable days, during which he suffered a good deal, and then at last one afternoon, with no small amount of nervousness, he made his confession.

"I've a nasty suspicion, Helstone, that I shouldn't be here," he said abruptly that day to Godfrey.

He was sitting as he began to speak in his friend's study, and Rita happened by an unusual chance to be out of the way. Godfrey had been reading, and Jack had been reading too, but for the last ten minutes before he spoke he had set his book upon his knees, and had been gazing intently into the fire, engaged, to tell the truth, not without difficulty, in screwing up his courage to broach the subject of which his mind was full.

Godfrey looked up at Mr. Dallas's address.

149

"That's an old story, isn't it?" he said. "I thought we had dismissed it."

"It's by no means an old story," retorted Jack. "If you will listen to me I am afraid you will find it a very new, and perhaps not a pleasant, one. I say I'm troubled about being here—because of"— and here he gave a great gulp—"well,— because of Rita."

"Because of —what?" asked Godfrey, thinking he had not heard aright.

"Why, are you deaf, man? Don't you hear me say—of Rita!" cried Jack, giving way to his nervousness in a shout, the absurdity of which so struck him as he uttered it that he burst next moment into a laugh.

Mr. Helstone looked at him in a puzzled way.

"I don't understand you," he said.

Poor Jack took up the poker, and began to hammer at the fire.

"I don't know that I understand my self," he said. "I'm six-and-twenty years older than she is, and I don't suppose she'd have me, even if you didn't object; but I can't get her out of my head—that's the fact of it. There now—the cat's out of the bag,—and the business is off my conscience, at any rate." And then, with unconscious vehemence, he stabbed the poker again into the middle of the coals.

There was complete silence after this speech. Godfrey sat with his eyes on his friend's face. He was so used to hear Jack talk nonsense that perhaps his first supposition was that he was talking non-sense now, but the look of grave and nervous earnestness with which Mr. Dallas sat and stared into the fire made it impossible for this impression to last many moments. When it gave way, however, Godfrey found himself almost speechless with surprise.

"Is it possible you are saying this seriously?" were the first words he gravely uttered.

"Seriously? God bless me, can't you see I am?" said Jack.

"And you mean that you care for— that you are—falling in love with Rita?"

"I'm not falling— I'm *fallen*," cried Jack. "The thing is done: it's no use talking about it. I'm only thinking now about her,—and you."

"I am afraid you have been very—imprudent," said Godfrey, rather hesitating over his final word. "As you say, it is hardly likely that, with such a difference in your ages—"

"I'm hanged if I know whether it's likely or not!" burst in Jack impetuously. "As far as that goes I must take my chance. But I'm in your hands, you see. I can't speak to her if you're against it,— and I'm not such a fool as to think you will like me to speak,—and yet, Helstone," he said with more self-control, "I do entreat you to let me do it. If you are right, and she won't have anything to say to me, then there's no harm done. But if by chance it should turn out that she liked me enough—" Poor Jack got so far, and then broke off, with a quiver in his voice.

"You know you have taken me immensely by surprise," Godfrey said gravely, after another brief silence. "I think that unequal marriages, such as this would be, are far from desirable ; but of course, except for the

153

difference in your ages, I could have no objection to make. In many respects—in every respect except that one— But don't move in the matter hastily, Jack," he interrupted himself earnestly. "You have taken me so aback that I hardly know what to say to you; and I don't feel convinced by any means yet that you know your own mind."

"No, I don't suppose you do," replied Jack rather meekly. And then he walked twice up and down the room, and finally paused in front of his friend's chair. "I know you wouldn't have chosen me for her," he said abruptly; "but—suppose she likes me better than you think?"

"Well?" said Godfrey.

"Well—would you let me have her?"

"I imagine," said Godfrey, after a few moments' silence, but he spoke rather lugubriously—"I imagine in that case that it would not be very easy for me to do anything else."

The colour came rather hotly into Jack's face. "Now it's an odd thing," he said. "I've lived for forty-four years in the world, and I've seen women enough, heaven knows, and yet I never wanted to marry one of them till I came across this little girl of yours. I don't know what there is in her—upon my word I don't; but I'd go through fire and water for her. There's not a young fellow living who would love her better than I will—if she ever gives me the chance."

"My dear Jack," said Mr. Helstone, rather uneasily, "I think if you had told me of this sooner, I would—somehow or other—have got you back to town."

"Ah, so you're coming to my view of

that matter at last, are you?" replied Jack, with a laugh that had, however, rather a grim tone in it.

On the day this talk between the two friends took place, Mr. Dallas had been pronounced almost fit for travelling. He was not well yet, but Dr. Carson had told him that he might count on going home in another week. "So you will get me off your hands next Tuesday—at last," Jack had said to Rita, and she had tried to make some light reply, but the poor little lips had trembled and almost failed.

For, though Rita did not quite know what had happened to her, she was conscious that a time that had made her very happy was coming to an end, and the prospect of this ending was troubling and saddening her. No termination of a pleasure had ever saddened her in the same way before. She did not understand the sadness and restlessness that she felt, nor what made her cling with such increasing eagerness to the performance of those various little services that it had been her pleasure to do for Mr. Dallas during these happy weeks.

"You will be having a royal time of it soon now," he had said to her this morning with a laugh, and she had turned away and could not answer him. A royal time— when he was gone! Did he think that? Was that all he knew? she had cried almost passionately to herself.

Mr. Dallas was unusually quiet during the hours that followed his talk with Godfrey. Rita had been out while that talk went on, but she came home in the dusk, and met Jack on the stairs as she went up to her own room.

"I am glad you have come back," he stopped to tell her.

"So am I!" she answered brightly. "I am generally glad." And then he exclaimed, "What a blessed thing!" and passed on, without listening to her explanation, and at that moment she did not perceive that he was more grave than usual.

As the evening passed on, however, she could not but become aware that he talked less than he generally did, and indulged in silences that were not customary with him.

"Are you tired?" she asked him a little timidly once, making some excuse for going towards him; but he looked up at her, and smiled, and shook his head.

"No, I am only thinking," he answered. "I am thinking of my deserts,—and it makes me a little melancholy, for I have not deserved much, I am afraid. Do you think I have?"

"In what way?" she asked hesitating. "I don't quite understand."

"In the way of happiness," he said. "What we all want is to be happy—isn't it? but if I am not good enough to be allowed to be happy—?"

"Oh, but I hope you are good!" she said quickly. And then, as if she was ashamed of the tone in which she had spoken, she coloured vividly and turned away.

"You must do more than *hope* that, dear. You must believe it too," he said a moment afterwards below his breath. But she did not hear that response.

He was out of spirits, she thought, and the poor little maiden in her half-childish heart wished she could cheer him, and yearned for the power to comfort him that she did not know she had. In a little while he would be all alone, she thought with pain. "Oh, it is hard to get to like people and then be obliged to part from them!" she cried to herself, feeling as if at his going her very heart would bleed.

"Even papa seems sorry," she reflected. "Everybody has got so dull to-day, since Dr. Carson said that Mr. Dallas might go." And she thought in all simplicity that her father was indeed mourning over his friend's approaching departure, when it was in truth something far more closely affecting his own happiness that was causing the depression which clouded Godfrey's brow, and kept his lips closed. "How in the world can Jack Dallas have made himself such a fool?" was in fact the thought that was in Mr. Helstone's mind a dozen times to-night, and he felt sore and injured, as perhaps a man may be excused for doing in the first moments of discovering that another man has set his heart on robbing him of his only daughter.

This evening that followed Jack's confession was not pleasant to Jack himself, nor to Godfrey, nor to Rita, and the days that followed it were hardly more satisfactory. Godfrey had scarcely given his consent that Mr. Dallas should speak to Rita, but yet, if he had not given it, neither had he refused it, and Jack understood probably that he was left at liberty to speak if he pleased ; and yet day after day went past, and he still held his peace. In fact he was afraid to speak, as he confessed later on. " I tried to do it half-a-dozen times," he declared, " but when I opened my lips my tongue clove to the roof of my mouth,

and the most horrible tremors ran down my
spine. Of course I shouldn't have had any
tremors if I had been twenty years younger,
but it's no joke, I can tell you, for a man
of four-and-forty to offer himself to a girl
of eighteen. I'm blest if any consideration
should ever make me do it again! I nearly
made up my mind more than once to give
the whole thing up and go back to town."

But of course, though he said this, Jack
did not go back to town till the question
he wanted to put to Rita was asked and
answered.

He put off asking it, however, from day
to day, and during these days he per-
plexed and disturbed poor little Rita not
a little by his irregularities of mood and
temper. He treated her differently from
how he had treated her before, and she
did not know what made him different;

he was sometimes very tender to her, and
at other times he was grave and cold, and
when he was tender she was very happy,
and when he was cold her poor little heart
sank. They had been such delightful weeks
while he was getting better; what was the
matter with this week, she asked herself,
that it had become so unlike the rest?
She was observant enough, and she saw
not only that Mr. Dallas was changed
towards herself, but that in his relations
with her father there was a difference too.
The two men kept more apart, and when
they were together Jack no longer talked
and jested in his ordinary light-hearted
way; their intercourse with one another had
become grave, and Rita, sympathetically,
became grave too, and anxious, and troubled.
She had a feeling that something had happened, but she did not like to ask what
163

it was; perhaps some shy self-consciousness kept her from asking.

And so, not very happily, the days went on until that one came which it had been settled was to be the last of Mr. Dallas's visit; and then at last Jack spoke.

He was in the dining-room after lunch alone with Rita. She had been sitting working (sitting at a distance from him, and wondering, poor little soul, why he did not care to come nearer to her, or to speak to her); he had been trying to read; for half-an-hour they had neither of them uttered a word, when at length he threw down his book, and, rising with a start from his chair, went up to her.

"Now I ought to be packing," he said abruptly, "but I can't go and pack till I've said a word to you. And I am going to say something that perhaps may keep

you from ever being the same to me again,
—and yet, though I know that, I must say
it. I suppose you guess what it is, Rita?
you guess how I've got to like you?—though
I'm as old as your father, and though you
think me a fool, I dare say, ever to imagine
you could care for me. But, my dear,
I've been thinking of it this way—Just
let me tell you. You have been so sweet
and good to me that I can't help thinking
you have a little liking for me in a way,
and what I am thinking is, that we Dallases
are not very long lived, and if I were off
the scene, say even twenty years after
this, you would still be a young woman,
and might marry somebody else,—and so,
taking that into account, if you could make
up your mind to come to me—? My dear
little girl, I know I'm asking you to give
your youth to me, and I've no right to do

that,—it strikes me horribly that I'm a selfish brute altogether,—only you've made me care for you as I never cared for anybody else in my life, and though, perhaps, the whole thing may strike you as ludicrous—"

But Jack stopped abruptly here, for all at once a little cry came from Rita.

"Oh, Mr. Dallas!" she said. "Oh—oh—don't say such things!"

"Such things as that I want you to marry me?" inquired Jack.

"N—o, not that. At least— Oh," cried Rita tremulously, "I could never dare!"

"You couldn't dare to marry me! God bless you, my darling," exclaimed Jack in delight, "if you are willing to do it, what should hinder you?"

And then he sat down beside her, and seeing her hand very near to him, he ventured after a moment to take it into his, and when he found that she submitted to this proceeding his courage began to rise apace.

"What in the world should make you say that you couldn't dare? If you are willing to do it, why shouldn't you dare?" he repeated.

"Oh, because I am not fit," pleaded poor little Rita breathlessly. "Everybody would say so. Oh," almost with a gasp, "I don't know *what* papa would say!"

"But *I* do," answered Jack confidently. "He says—"

"Do you mean that you have spoken to him?" and Rita opened her frightened eyes wide.

"Yes, of course I have; and what he says is—'It's a pity you are not younger, but if she likes to take you it can't be helped.'"

"Does he? Are you speaking the truth?" asked Rita, hardly above her breath.

"The literal truth!"

"Oh, I—I am glad of that!" And Rita gave a sigh of relief. "But all the same," she added timidly and trembling, next moment, "I would rather not."

And then she raised a wistful look to Jack's face, and suddenly made an effort, which was quite vain, to take her hand away.

"Now, what do you mean by telling me you would rather not?" he said. He looked rather uncomfortable, as if he was conscious of not being at home in these novel circumstances; and as for her, she seemed less at home in them even than he.

"I mean, I don't think I could. I—I shouldn't like it," she said very shyly.

"You couldn't imagine me as your husband, you mean?"

"No," she said.

"But you haven't tried?"

"N—o," she repeated in a troubled way.

"Well, but I want you to try. My dear, unless you do you can't tell."

"But—it seems wrong," she said faintly.

"Wrong—to care for me? Why? Because you don't think I deserve to be cared for?"

"Oh, no!"—very emphatically.

"Then you must explain yourself."

But of course when he told her to explain herself she did not say a word; she only sat quite still, with her face turned away.

"Well," he exclaimed resignedly after a little silence, "if you will really say nothing more I suppose I must give it up. Must I? and go back to my solitude?"

"Oh!" she said, quivering.

"It's an awful disappointment to me," said Jack with a heavy sigh. "However, I suppose I deserved it for supposing that any girl could care for me—now."

And then he dropped her hand, and seemed just about to get up from his seat, when she began to cry.

"Oh, don't! How can you?" she sobbed out reproachfully, "when you know —when anybody might know— Oh, to say I couldn't care for you!" and she turned to him, and the poor little forsaken hand went pitifully holding itself out to him again, till he took it back and clasped it closer than before.

"Then you don't mean what you have been saying?" he asked her joyfully.

170

"I—don't know," she answered almost below her breath.

"Well, but, you see, I must either go away, or else you must make up your mind to have me."

"I don't know what to do!" she said.

"Then let me settle it for you. You know, if I am to be your husband, you can't let me begin to settle things too soon. My little girl," Jack said suddenly, with a tone that she had never heard in his voice before, "you will come to me."

And then he took her into his arms, and wasted no further arguments upon her, but merely kissed her lips shut.

"You will never say that dreadful thing again, will you? what you said, I mean, about—about twenty years?" she asked him presently, turning to him, and looking into his face with eyes that seemed ready to fill again with tears.

But Jack at this inquiry burst out laughing. He was triumphantly happy, and could afford to make a jest of what he had told her in almost grim earnest half-an-hour before.

CHAPTER VII.

MRS. HELSTONE and Miss Taylor were a good deal shocked, but Godfrey gravely kissed his daughter, and merely told her that if she liked Jack there was nothing more to be said. For his own part, the prospect before him was not a very bright one. With Rita gone from him his house would be lonely enough.

"I think I shall shut it up for a time," he said to his mother, "and go abroad."

Two years ago, at Margaret's death, Mrs. Helstone had decided that she would not accept the offer Godfrey made her of taking her daughter-in-law's empty place at Ivor.

She was growing old, and the charge of the large establishment there would have been a burden to her. So she had remained at the Dene, and at the Dene, even after her granddaughter should be gone away, she still proposed to stay.

When Rita became engaged it was the middle of February, and her marriage, it was presently decided, should take place in June.

"But she must come up to town before that," said Jack. "She will want to come for her marriage gown, and *I* shall want her for my own satisfaction. So make up your minds to come, all three of you. She will need Miss Taylor to help her to buy her finery. I shall expect you to come for a month or six weeks at any rate."

"Well, we'll see about that," answered Godfrey, and the result was that in April they went.

174

It was a mild, bright spring, and London, of course, to Rita's eyes, looked as it had never looked before.

"I sometimes have qualms about bringing you to live here," Jack said to her; but she on her side had naturally neither qualms nor regrets. She was as happy as the days were long, and Jack was equally happy on his side. He had begun to play the *rôle* of lover rather late in life, but he played it with very fair success in spite of that.

They went about a great deal, for they had sights to see, and a house to look for, and Rita had acquaintances to make. Mr. Dallas had few relations, but he had many friends, and to some of them he was eager to introduce his future wife. "You may as well get to know them now," he said, "for it will give you more of a home feeling when you come back to live

amongst them." So the introductions
were made, and led naturally to invita-
tions, and Rita's time was soon well filled.

She had never been much in London
before this, and she looked on everything
with fresh eyes of pleasure that gave an
endless delight and entertainment to Jack.
He was so much in love that he spent
almost all his time at her side. If he
had been five-and-twenty he could not
have been more absorbed in her, nor could
he have been, nor have made her, happier.

Her new position towards him had
affected her rather seriously at the beginning. It had seemed to her such an
astonishing fact that they could be engaged to one another, that she had hardly
known at first how to comport herself
towards him; she was less at ease with
him for a time than she had been before

he made his proposal; she showed herself shy at being left alone with him; she could not bring her tongue to call him anything but "Mr. Dallas."

"Oh, I couldn't say anything else; I *couldn't* say 'Jack'!" she declared. If he had had any other name she might have managed to utter it, she thought, but to address him as "Jack"!—the very thought brought the colour to her face.

"Well, but you must do it, sooner or later," he urged. "Come, do it now, and break the ice at once."

But she only laughed and would not, and she had been engaged to him for a week before he first heard his name from her lips.

In fact, though in the early days of their acquaintance she had expressed stern opinions sometimes about his boyishness, and had taken upon herself not unfrequently to rebuke him for his faults and his various shortcomings, in her heart, now that she was about to become his wife, Rita entertained a boundless respect and admiration for her lover—such a respect that she could not bear to set herself on the same level with him, but delighted in believing that in everything he was better than herself.

"I think that when girls fall in love with people who are quite young it can't be anything like—this," she said simply to him once. "It can't be half so good, I mean. I wouldn't have you younger than you are if I could choose. You are quite young enough. A boy and girl together must be so—silly."

"And we are always wise, of course," replied Jack. Upon which she laughed and blushed.

178

"We are not always wise, I know; but yet—it's different," she said with emphasis.

He was pretty well as proud of her as a man could be, though he laughed at himself for his delight in her not a little. "I suppose I am a fool," he said one day to an intimate friend of his, but when he spoke so he only did it, I am of opinion, that he might enjoy his friend's contradiction. For the lady—a Mrs. Lomas—to whom he made this speech was a motherly woman who had a great regard for him, and who also, from her first introduction to Rita, had taken a liking to her too. She showed Rita much kindness during her stay in town, and did not a little for her entertainment.

Mrs. Lomas was very bright and kindly and social. She took Rita to several parties, where the little country girl enjoyed herself moderately, and one day she gave a great entertainment specially in her honour at her own house. "I want to introduce you to a number of people, my dear," she told her, "very nice people that it will be good for you to know." And though Rita felt rather nervous at the prospect of it—for the world of London was very new to her, and she was pretty shy of it as yet—the party was arranged, and one bright May afternoon Mrs. Lomas gathered a hundred or so of her acquaintances together at her house at Hampstead.

It was a sunny, summer-like day. The house stood in large gardens, and, early in the season though it was, the guests spread themselves over the lawns, and an abundance of colour and sunshine and music made the scene very gay. So pretty a garden-party Rita had rarely before been present at, and she herself, though she was unconscious of the fact, was one of the prettiest portions of it. Mrs. Lomas had helped her to choose her dress, or rather had entirely suggested it, and it had proved so great a success that Jack, when he saw her, said no woman had ever been so perfectly attired before. "You look like a young goddess,—a sweet young Hebe," he told her, with an extravagant praise that she laughed at, but yet perhaps liked to hear.

There was perhaps no great enjoyment to Godfrey in these gatherings to which circumstances forced him to accompany his daughter. If he had ever cared much for entertainments of the sort, his relish for them had died out long ago; he had few friends in London, and not even many acquaintances, nor did he much desire to increase their number. It was with

181

resignation rather than pleasure that he
took Rita to her dances and parties. Sometimes he shifted the labour on Miss Taylor's
shoulders. To-day he had been half re-
solved to stay at home ; had the day been
less tempting a one perhaps he would have
done so. But the sun shone, and the drive
to Hampstead promised to be pleasant,
and so when Rita begged him to go with
them he went.

"I suppose we shall get away by seven
o'clock or so," he said when they were
starting.

"Y—es, unless— They sometimes dance,"
suggested Rita insinuatingly.

And then, with that resignation which
he had learnt, Godfrey got into the carriage
and held his peace.

He was not much burdened with the
charge of Rita after they had once reached

their destination, for Mrs. Lomas took her immediately off his hands, and he was left at liberty to wander where he pleased. So he talked to such few acquaintances as he found, and rambled about the grounds, with or without a companion, and yawned a little perhaps, now and then, as the afternoon slowly passed away.

After, however, a couple of hours or so had elapsed an incident occurred which had at least the effect of dissipating his weariness very effectually. He was standing alone, looking on rather indifferently at the scene before him, when he saw Mr. Dallas hastening towards him with a decision that seemed to him to imply some special object in his approach, nor was he mistaken, for as soon as Jack had come near enough to speak, he made an announcement that sent the blood suddenly through Godfrey's veins.

"I say, Helstone," he exclaimed, "look out! There's Joanne Beresford somewhere about the place."

"Joanne Beresford!" echoed Godfrey, as if his friend had uttered the name of a ghost.

"Yes; I've seen her; I saw her five minutes ago. I can't stop now to look her up," cried Jack, "but I thought you'd like to know."

"Do you mean that you have *spoken* to her?" asked Godfrey almost incredulously.

"No, I haven't spoken to her," answered Jack, "but I've seen her. I knew her in a moment almost, but to make sure I asked Mrs. Lomas. I should have spoken, of course, only I didn't like to do it till I was certain, and then she had got out of sight. But you'll find her in a minute if you try. She's got on a black dress."

"I'll look for her," said Godfrey instantly. He felt curiously braced all at once, as if he had drunk some powerful stimulant. Without another word he parted from Jack, and went straight to where the throng of men and women was thickest. Surely if Jack had known her at once, he thought, *he* should know her too. But he searched for her for a good while in vain, and he was getting impatient and beginning to think that he would go and seek for Mrs. Lomas's assistance, when suddenly, face to face with him, he saw some one standing whom he looked at for a moment or two, and then with a strange thrill recognized.

He went up to her, and put out his hand.

"I am afraid you will hardly remember me?" he said.

But he had scarcely uttered the words

before he knew that she remembered him,
for her colour came with a force that
for the moment she evidently could not
check.

"I was hoping that I should see you.
I have been talking to your daughter.
She told me that you were here," she
replied.

"I heard of you only two minutes ago
from Jack Dallas," Godfrey answered.

"I haven't seen Mr. Dallas," she said,
"but Mrs. Lomas told me just now—"
And then she hesitated.

Godfrey, however, at once finished her
sentence.

"She told you, I suppose, that Rita and
he are going to be married? Yes; that
seems odd, doesn't it? In the old days we
should have been rather surprised if we had
been told that I should come to be his

186

father-in-law. But many a strange thing is brought about.—I am so glad to see you once more."

"And I am glad," she answered. She had already recovered her self-possession. The quick blood had gone back again, and she was looking at him now with her old calm directness, and with her old sweet eyes too. (How well he remembered them, he thought, across this long bridge of twenty years!)

"Let us sit down," he said. "I want to hear about your people. Come here into the shade. Now tell me first of all about your father."

"He is very well," she said brightly; "well and strong. He can walk ten miles still without being tired, and he preaches every Sunday,—and he is as fond of fishing as ever," she added laughing.

187

" It does one good to hear that," said Godfrey. " And Mrs. Beresford ? "

" Mamma is not quite so young as my father, but still she is fairly well too."

" And they are still in the old place ? How many of you are there with them ? What about yourself ? "

" Oh, I have always lived at home," she answered. " And Violet is at home too,— but she is a widow now. She lives with us, along with her two little girls. And my brother Tom is dead,—and Femie," she added after a moment in a lower voice.

" What, little Femie ? " he exclaimed regretfully.

" Yes, she died when she was fifteen. It was a terrible grief to us. Do you recollect what a dear little child she was ? Do you remember that first evening you spent with us," Joanne asked suddenly, "and how you carried her about the garden on your shoulders?"

"Yes, I remember," he said, with a flood of memories indeed rising as he spoke. "I remember; I have never forgotten her."

"They are nearly all of them married and scattered abroad, except these," she said after a moment's silence. "Dick and Harry are farming in Canada, and Victor is a soldier in the West Indies; and Felix is a clergyman, and has a living in the north; and Lilian and Edith are married here in London; and Maude is married at York. It is with Lilian that I am staying now. She has five children. There are a great many children amongst us altogether. Just think!" and she laughed—"I have eighteen nephews and nieces now."

"And *you* have never married!" he exclaimed abruptly.

"My sisters married very quickly, and mamma had a great deal on her hands. There has always been work for me at home," she said.

He had scarcely so far had time to arrange his thoughts; he scarcely knew yet, as she sat beside him, whether she did or did not seem to him like the Joanne Beresford of old. She was altered, of course, and perhaps the inevitable changes that these twenty years had made in her forced themselves on his notice more now than they would be likely to do at any future meeting he might have with her. He missed her lost youth, and was conscious that he missed it; he perceived expressions in her that were unfamiliar to him; but yet she was like enough to her old self make him presently say impulsively—

"I think I should have known you anywhere. Dallas had told me you were here, so I was looking for you, but I don't believe I should have passed you even without any warning."

"I knew you at once," she answered. "But then," she added, "I had been warned too."

"Mrs. Lomas introduced me to your daughter," she told him presently. "At first I never suspected who she was. I noticed the name, of course, because it is not a common one, but it was only after a little while, when she happened to speak of where she lived— You see I had remembered things you used to tell me, and when she said she lived in Gloucestershire, and spoke of Ivor, then I could not but know. But it seemed so strange; and strangest of all when Mrs. Lomas told me presently of her engagement to Mr. Dallas."

"Yes, he is twenty-six years her senior.

It is a pity," Godfrey said. " She is linking herself to a wrong generation. But still they seem fond enough of one another, Heaven knows."

He said the last words almost with a little acrimony, and Joanne laughed.

" You speak as if you suffered from their love-making," she said.

" I don't mean to say that I suffer from it," he answered. " I try to be very tolerant of it ; but I have nothing belonging to me but Rita,—or rather I had nothing but her three months ago, when this fellow came and took possession of her. I have nothing at all now."

" But you will have her future life to be an interest to you, and her children, probably," Joanne said.

" Yes," replied Godfrey, " I suppose so." But he did not speak with great warmth.

Perhaps as the minutes passed these two began to feel a little strange each with the other. Many a time Godfrey had longed almost passionately to see Joanne Beresford, and now he saw her, and he had no desire except to remain by her side; and yet the feeling with which he looked at her and listened to her was not, he was conscious, the feeling of former days. It was not that she disappointed him, for, if he had met her now for the first time, he told himself that he should call her a noble and lovable-looking woman; but she was changed, as he felt more and more, and it was this inevitable change that chilled him. She was not the Joanne that he had parted from that bitter day, when they had both been young.

He wondered if she felt the difference as keenly as he was beginning to do himself.

He met her eyes once fixed on his face, and he returned their gaze with rather a grave smile.

" I can hardly believe yet that we have met again," he said.

" No, it is such a long time—" she began to answer, and then did not end her sentence.

They had been together for half-an-hour, and each had asked and answered many questions; but now their first inquiries had become exhausted, and there were pauses coming in their talk, and perhaps the sense of strangeness in their renewed intercourse was pressing upon them both.

She looked at her watch at the half-hour's end and said, " I am afraid I must be going home. Lilian was to have come here with me, but she was prevented by a cold."

"How are you going?" he asked. "Have you a carriage?"

"Oh, no; I go by train," she said.

"Then I will walk to the station with you," he answered.

They both rose up, and she left him to make her way to Mrs. Lomas and bid good-bye to her. He went slowly towards the gate, and presently he heard her step behind him, and turned round and joined her again.

"It is a good many years since I had my last walk with you," he said to her as they turned into the road.

"Yes, a great many years," she answered gravely.

"Would your sister let me call upon her, I wonder?" he asked.

"She would be very glad, I am sure," Joanne cordially replied. "She lives in

Brook Street, No. —. But I am sorry," she added, hesitating for a moment, "that I shall not see you again."

"Why? Are you going away?" he asked quickly.

"Yes," she said; "this is my last day in town. I am going home to-morrow."

There was a pause after this. He made no comment on her answer. They were crossing a part of the Heath, and for a minute they walked over the grass in silence.

He was vexatiously conscious that the feeling of constraint between them was not growing less but more—that, with their first curiosity regarding one another satisfied, they seemed to have exhausted all that they had to say, and were being forced to fall back upon the ordinary commonplaces of ordinary acquaintances.

"It is a disappointment to me to hear that you are going so soon," he said abruptly after that little silence ; " but even to have seen you this once has been a great pleasure, and I hope, if not now, yet some other time— Do you know," he said, making a great effort to shake off his stiffness,— " do you know, I should dearly like some day to run down to Brentwood again."

"Should you?" she answered, as if half-doubtfully.

"It would give me such pleasure to shake hands with your father once more. I wish you would tell him so. Tell him that, long as I have been away, I hope to see him again yet."

"If you ever find time to come I am sure he will be very glad," Joanne said. But Godfrey thought she spoke rather coldly.

"You would not find the place much

altered," she went on, with a little hurry in her tone. "The inn has changed hands; your old landlord died a year or two ago; and there are a few new people in the village, but that is all. You remember my aunt?"

"Mrs. Arthur Beresford?" exclaimed Godfrey. "Indeed I *ought* to have remembered her, for she was very kind to me. I am ashamed of not having asked after her sooner."

"Oh, but she is dead," said Joanne.

"Is she dead?" cried Godfrey. "Dear me! she didn't look like a woman *to* die. And those pretty daughters?—at least one of them was very pretty."

"You mean Clara? Yes, she is very pretty. She married long ago. Three of them are married, and Fanny, the youngest one, lives here in town with Hugh."

"Ah, then has Hugh never got a wife ?" and Godfrey, with this question, giving a quick glance at his companion, saw, or thought he saw, her colour rise.

"No, he has no wife," she said. "But he and Fanny are very happy together. Fanny is a nice girl,—or rather *woman*, I should say," she corrected herself quickly, with a laugh. "But she is younger than I am."

"Yes, three or four years younger, I suppose," he said. "I remember her very well. She was about fifteen when I was at Brentwood, and she was very shy. You were nineteen that year, you know."

"Yes," she merely said.

Their talk did not flow easily, and yet when they reached the station and found that her train was due in a few minutes he was sorry. He went to the platform with her, and they sat down to wait. He wanted to say something more to her than he had yet said, but he felt strangely tongue-tied. He had been excited an hour ago when he met her first, but now he was not excited; his first emotion had given way to something that was almost coldness; he sat by her side and was conscious that his nearness to her did not stir him as in thought, during these years that they had been apart, he had believed, if he should ever meet her again, it would do.

They heard the whistle of the approaching train, and she rose up in silence.

"Now you must go, and we seem to have had no talk yet," he said suddenly.

"Oh yes, we have had a little. I am glad to have seen you," she replied.

But though she said she was glad, to Godfrey's ears, made sensitive perhaps by his own consciousness of inability to rise to the occasion, her voice seemed to have a tone of sadness in it. He opened the door of an empty carriage for her, and she took her seat, and then, standing at the door, he put out his hand to her.

"I wish I had told them not to wait for me, and I would have seen you home," he said all at once.

"Oh, I am accustomed to go about alone," she answered with a smile.

"I dare say you are, but I was thinking of the gain to myself. I am sorry to bid you good-bye," he said.

He had kept her hand for a few moments in his. Standing face to face with her, and looking into the eyes that had once been so dear to him, he was feeling keenly that he had wasted this short hour. It seemed to him that, if he could stay with her now, he could talk differently to her. But the doors of the carriages were being rapidly closed, and she was withdrawing her hand. With a sudden impulse at the last moment he said, "God bless you!" And then he took off his hat, and remained uncovered till the train had swept away.

Slowly, and with an acute feeling of dissatisfaction and regret, he retraced his steps after this to Mrs. Lomas's. With Joanne Beresford at his side he had felt dull and cold, but now with her gone he began to long for her presence again, and to be enraged at himself for his temporary indifference. "I was stunned,—I suppose that is the truth of it," he told himself. "But she must have thought I had forgotten everything. I scarcely even told her I was sorry she was leaving town. Well,—I have been a fool." And he returned to his party ill enough pleased.

He searched for his daughter, and found her presently blooming and happy.

"They *are* going to dance," she informed him joyfully, as soon as he joined her. "I was wondering where you were. You seem to have been out of sight such a long time. And, oh, did you see Miss Beresford?" cried Rita, trying to ask her question quite naturally, but yet feeling a little conscious as she asked it, for Jack in these days, as might be supposed, was not very reticent, and had told her something more about Joanne Beresford than she had known of old.

"Yes, I have seen her," Godfrey answered calmly, "and I am glad you saw her too."

"She talked to me for a good while. I thought she was very nice," Rita said rather

203

shyly. "And how pretty she is! I should never have guessed she was so old."

"Do you call her old? She is thirty-nine. People often keep their good looks longer than that, my dear," Godfrey replied.

"Oh, you did find her then?" said Jack coming up. "I wanted to go in search of you, for I should like to have shaken hands with her too, but Mrs. Hetherington got hold of me, and I couldn't break away. Well, and what did you think of her? She is altered, of course, but by the glance I had of her she seemed to me to be looking wonderfully well."

"Yes, she is altered; we all are, I suppose," Godfrey answered with a half-laugh.

"I haven't the least doubt *I* am," replied Jack. "We all wore our hair in hyacinth-ine curls, for instance, when she saw us last. I remember that fact. Just think, Rita! It clustered over our temples, and descended on our coat collars."

"I think it must have been very nice," said Rita,—"far nicer than as you wear it now."

"Well, it was certainly *different*, at any rate, and there's no doubt your father looked a much showier person when Miss Beresford knew him before than he does to-day. Indeed, to tell the truth," said Jack, with a mischievous twinkle in his eye, "I've no doubt she must have thought him a good deal changed for the worse, for he was a good-looking fellow in those days, though perhaps you would scarcely believe it now."

"Yes, you *think* I find that hard to believe!" cried Rita, with a little proud laugh.

The dancers fell presently to their work, and Godfrey looked at them for a while, and then strolled away. He could think of nothing but Joanne Beresford. That paralysis of feeling that had come over him for a time in her presence had passed away now, and his mind occupied itself unceasingly in trying to recall all she had said, and each look of the half-familiar, half-unknown face.

"I was an idiot to be startled because she was changed," he told himself impatiently. "How, by any mortal possibility, could she have helped being changed? And as for her manner,—that was simply what I made it. I believe she would have been cordial and frank enough if I had allowed her, but I gave her no chance. I have been a fool!" he repeated. But if he had been a fool he could not now undo his folly.

206

"Papa, dear, are you tired?" Rita said tenderly to him presently as they drove home. "I am afraid it has all been rather dull for you, though *I* have thought it delightful. Hasn't it been delightful, Jack?" And then she turned eagerly to her lover, and Mr. Helstone did not find that he was called upon to answer the question she had asked.

So they drove to their hotel through the lighted streets, and Godfrey held his peace, and, leaning back in the corner of his carriage, thought with half-involuntary persistency of the woman he had loved, and had seen again after so many years.

CHAPTER VIII.

THE Helstones returned home at the end
of May, for Rita's marriage was of course
to take place at Ivor; and on the 20th of
June the little damsel put on her orange
blossoms with a mixture of trepidation and
devout rejoicing, and entered upon her
new life.

It was not a very bright day to Godfrey.
" Dearest old father, I think you will have
to come and live with us," the girl had begun
to say to him during the weeks before her
wedding; but though she looked forward to
this arrangement, it was hardly one perhaps
that presented itself to Mr. Helstone him-

self as very probable. "I will go away from Ivor for a time at any rate," was all he would promise her. "Perhaps I shall go abroad. I can't tell you yet."

"But *why* can't you tell me?" she urged him more than once. Though she urged him, however, she could not get him to say anything more.

The joy bells rang on her marriage day, and the sun shone, and she cried a little, but she was very happy. As for Mr. Dallas, he was so nervous that, as he protested afterwards, when he came into church his knees knocked together. "You see," he explained to Rita, "it was such a mistake of mine not to accustom myself to the ceremony in my youth."

They were going to Switzerland, and they started as soon as the wedding breakfast was over.

"There's not a happier man treading the earth than I am to-day," Mr. Dallas said to Godfrey as he bade good-bye to him ; "and, God helping me, I'll try to make and keep my little girl happy too."

"I believe you will," Godfrey answered briefly.

He kissed his daughter, and Jack wrung his hand, and then the carriage door was closed, and the young wife, and *not* young husband, went their way.

"I am coming home to you, mother," Godfrey said to Mrs. Helstone when all the guests were gone ; and so they went together to the Dene, and spent their quiet evening there.

"I couldn't stand any more of the place just now," he said, as they sat talking after dinner. "I had been thinking of shutting it up, you know, but it struck me only

yesterday, that instead of shutting it up I
might ask Miss Taylor to stay and take
charge of it; so I have asked her, and she
will do that, and have her sister with her
for company. Perhaps I may come back
to it again before long; I can't tell yet."

Godfrey spent a few days between Ivor
and the Dene, doing work and making
arrangements of various kinds, and then
rather abruptly he said to Mrs. Helstone
one evening—

"I am thinking of going for a week or
two into Derbyshire. You remember that
place, Brentwood, where Jack and I were
long ago? Old Beresford is still vicar there,
and I should like to go and see him and his
people."

"Indeed!" she answered quickly.

She could not but look keenly at
her son, trying and wishing to read his

thoughts. It was many a year since the Beresfords' name had been spoken between them, but she was not likely to have forgotten what she had once known about Joanne.

"What has made you think of that? Have you heard anything about them of late?" she asked after a moment or two's silence. And then—for he had been prepared for some such question—he told her in a few words how he had met "one of the daughters" when he was in town. Which daughter it had been he did not say, and Mrs. Helstone longed to ask, but did not.

Perhaps she gave a little inward sigh, but after he had announced his intention she said nothing to try to dissuade him from carrying it out. If he meant to go back to his old love she could not hinder him, she knew. She had not the power to do that, nor perhaps almost the desire; for during the years of Godfrey's marriage Mrs. Helstone had come silently to recognize with tolerable clearness that the burden laid upon her son had not been easy to bear, but that it had been one which had eaten into his life, and made him a different man from what in her early proud anticipations she had hoped that he would be. That poor dead woman had been a faithful and loving wife to him; but no one knew better than Mrs. Helstone did now that no joy, and no quickening of any power that he possessed (but only the reverse of that), had come to him from his marriage with her. She was in her grave now, and Rita had gone to another home, and Godfrey was almost a young man still. "If he wants to marry again I will not try to prevent him," Mrs. Helstone thought.

"I am afraid it is hardly wise to go back to a woman whom he has not seen for twenty years (if that is indeed what is in his mind), but I must leave it all alone. I cannot help him, and if I speak I may vex him." So she said nothing more, and Godfrey was grateful for her silence.

He lingered at Ivor for a week or two, delaying his final decision about his journey from day to day. "Shall I go?" he asked himself again and again. "If I go, shall I not find her changed in a hundred ways?" But yet, though he feared and almost believed that he should find her changed, in the end his desire to see her once more proved stronger than his fear.

So one morning at last he said good-bye to his mother and started for Brentwood. "I shall probably be back again in a week or two," he told Mrs. Helstone.

214

She made no comment on this announcement. "God bless you, my dear," she merely said when he went, with a little quiver in her voice that perhaps did not catch his ear.

In the sunny summer evening Godfrey—almost the only passenger who stopped there—got down at the little country station that he had known once so well, and, ordering his things to be sent up to the inn, walked towards the village. It was all as quiet and sleepy-looking as of old. A few passers-by were in the street, but he saw no face that he recognized. A new landlord, as Joanne had told him, had taken Mr. Turnbull's place at the little inn.

He ordered some dinner, and waited while they got it ready for him. It was six o'clock, and when his meal was ended he meant to go up to the Vicarage. Perhaps he should not find Joanne at home, he suddenly thought. It was possible enough, with so many sisters married, and in all likelihood often wanting her. "Well, in that case I cannot help it," he told himself. "I shall see the Vicar at any rate." And scarcely knowing whether or not, if he learnt that she was absent, he should feel the disappointment much, he rose when his dinner was over, and putting on his hat, turned his steps towards the familiar road along which he had passed so many times of old.

His mood hitherto perhaps since he started on his journey had not been an eager one; perhaps he had been afraid of indulging in hopes that might end so soon in disappointment; "for to attempt to revive a state of feeling that has been set aside for twenty years," he had said to himself ever since he had left his own house, " is not, I fear, the effort of a wise man." But now, though he had been able so far to retain his calm self-possession, it broke down at last. His heart began to beat fast as he went along that well-remembered road; a hundred recollections came back to him. As he turned in at the Vicarage gate, and went through the winding walk that led out on the lawn, he felt as if it had only been yesterday that he had been there last—as if his life were still before him, and he and Joanne were still young.

And indeed it was difficult to believe that so many years had really passed away, for the same children's voices that he had been used to hear seemed to be in the air again as he approached the house, the

same figures he had known (he could almost
think) were moving about the lawn. For
a minute he stood still in the shadow of
the trees, and looked before him. Four
boys and girls, with half-familiar faces, were
playing tennis on the grass, while the hale
old Vicar stood and watched them, his feet
in their old fashion firmly planted well
apart, his hands behind his back, his hair
a little whiter than when Godfrey had seen
it last, his figure perhaps a little less erect,
but the voice as mellow and full as ever,
as at intervals he called out comments
on the game, or commendations to the
players.

Godfrey looked at the scene for a minute,
and then came forward into the sunshine,
causing the Vicar swiftly to change the
direction of his gaze. He went straight up
to the old man, and held out his hand.

"It is a long time since I saw you last, Mr. Beresford," he said.

The Vicar stood still and looked at him.

"Ah?" he said interrogatively. "Why, let me see! you are—you are—?" And then his look of inquiry changed, and the fine old face blazed into sudden recognition. "God bless my heart, you are young Helstone!" he cried, with a shout that made Godfrey laugh.

"I thought I should have puzzled you longer," he said.

"Not you, not you!" exclaimed the Vicar cheerily. "I've not a bad memory for faces. Besides, didn't you send a message to me? I heard of you from Joanne, you know. She said you talked of coming to see us again,—though, to tell the truth, I didn't pay much heed to that! But I'm glad to see you; you're welcome back.

219

Come away and speak to the old wife.
Joanne is somewhere about. And Edith
is here too, with her boys. There they
are—two stout little lads. And these slips
of girls are Vi's. You heard of poor Vi's
trouble, did you? Ah, yes, there have
been changes amongst us—many changes
since we met last," and his face saddened
for a moment ; " but, thank God, He has
left us more than He has taken away.
You have had your own sorrow too, Mr.
Helstone. Yes, yes, I heard about it.
Weil, you have felt what I have not felt
yet. We have borne what we have had
to bear together, my wife and I,—so far.
So far," he repeated, with a fall in his voice
that did not escape the other's ear.

They went towards the house, but before
they had reached it the Vicar threw his
head over his shoulder and stopped.

"Joanne, come here!" he cried suddenly, with one of his old stentorian calls; and Godfrey turned with a thrill, to find the woman he had come to seek only a few yards from him.

She was coming towards them along the gravel walk. He went hastily forward and met her. "Good God, can it be twenty years ago?" he thought.

She gave him her hand with a smile, but something of his own emotion seemed to be felt by her too, for she was not quick to speak.

"I told you, you know, that I should come," he was the first to say.

"Yes, you said you would like to come," she answered; "but one would like to do so many things—that never get done.—And so your daughter is married?" she added hastily, as if to

221

keep him from replying to her first sentence.

"Ay, ay, you've been getting a daughter married too, I hear," the Vicar struck in, "and married, of all men, to Jack Dallas! I thought it was a joke at first when Joanne told me. But he was a fine fellow—he was as fine a young fellow as I've often come across; and if he has got a good wife, I think your daughter, in spite of his years, has got a good husband. Mrs. Beresford thinks so, at any rate, I can tell you."

"Mrs. Beresford always did Jack justice," Godfrey answered laughing.

They found the old lady within-doors, looking more changed by a good deal, Godfrey thought, than the Vicar did. Her face had grown rather pinched, and she had got deaf, and her old activity was gone. But she had all her wits about her still.

"Mr. Helstone ? Is this Mr. Helstone ?" she said, looking him over from head to foot when they had said his name in her ear. "Ah well, I dare say it is, but I shouldn't have known him. It was Mr. Dallas that I always knew best. And he has just got married to your daughter, hasn't he ? Dear, dear, that did surprise me ! I'm very glad to see you again, Mr. Helstone ; and when you write to your friend give him my love, and tell him I'm an old woman now, but I've not forgotten him, and I wish him every happiness. You will do that, won't you ?"

"Yes, certainly I will," replied Godfrey heartily.

He sat down by her side, and presently the Vicar and Joanne came and sat down too. The young ones were still busy with their game upon the lawn, and these four,

who were no longer young, stayed together
for a long time, and talked of the years
that they had left behind. It was a quiet
hour, and one that had had no counterpart
in the days that had been of old, but its
grave friendliness was pleasant to Godfrey;
its tone seemed to imply that those old
days, brief as they had been, had linked
him to these companions with a tie that
long separation had not broken.

The one who said the most was Mr.
Beresford; the most silent of the four was
Joanne; but while her father talked the
consciousness of her presence seemed to
Godfrey almost to satisfy him. She was
working, and for minutes together he let
his eyes rest on her. Surely she was less
changed than he had supposed at first? he
began to think. Her face, that had seemed
half strange a month ago, was acquiring a

new familiarity to him now; he imagined
that he was seeing her again as she used
to be, not recognizing (perhaps because he
did not wish to recognize) that his former
memory of her was growing indistinct, half
effaced by the visible fact of what she had
become. By the time that the evening
ended he had said with satisfaction to
himself, "She only looks a very little
older; in everything else she is scarcely
changed at all."

They sat and talked till the door at last
opened briskly, and some one whom at first
Godfrey did not recognize stood for a
moment on the threshold, and then came
forward with an exclamation and a laugh.
She was a lady of pretty ample proportions,
dressed for walking, with bright dark eyes,
and a plump white hand, which she extended
instantly to Godfrey with much friendliness.

"Do you mean to say that you don't know me?" she asked, reading no doubt a certain hesitation in his manner as he rose to respond to her greeting. "Oh, that's dreadful! Why, I knew *you* merely by seeing you through the window. But, oh dear, it does change one so awfully to get fat!"

"I beg your pardon! Of course you are Miss Edith," Godfrey said; "or rather, I mean—" And then he had to stop, for he could not recall her married name.

"You mean 'Mrs. Travers,'" said Edith, giving him the information promptly. "Well, how funny it is to see you again! But, dear me, it's nice! Is it not, mother?" and she raised her voice into a higher key. "You like to see Mr. Helstone again, don't you?"

"Yes; but I should like better still to

see Mr. Dallas," replied Mrs. Beresford, with all her old downright frankness.

Mrs. Travers's advent broke up their quiet party.

"It is such a lovely evening; why do you all sit in here?" she asked. "Come out, Mr. Helstone, and have a walk with me in the garden. I want to ask you ever so many things, but I am not going to talk in this close room. Come along; it's so nice out of doors."

And so she carried him out, and in another minute he found himself walking along one of the well-remembered walks by her side.

"It makes one feel terribly old to see you again!" she exclaimed, as soon as she had got him here. "Not that I mean *you* look old, for you don't; I think you look very well; but it is so many years ago, and some of us are changed so much, and some— Ah, you know about little Femie, don't you?" and she shook her head and sighed. "That was a dreadful grief. Papa will never quite get over it—never, I believe. Isn't it rather sad to find us all so scattered, and all of us girls married, except Joanne? I don't know why Joanne hasn't married too. She might have done it, of course, if she had liked; or she might do it still to-morrow, if she would have poor Hugh. Oh, Mr. Helstone, do you remember Hugh?" and Edith burst out laughing. "I am sure there never was such a faithful old fellow. I always tell Joanne that she ought to take him still, just to reward him for his fidelity."

"Oh, I don't know about that," ejaculated Godfrey rather quickly. "Fidelity is best left sometimes to be its own reward.

I dare say Mr. Hugh Beresford is very happy."

"Well, certainly I can't say he is *un*happy," Mrs. Travers acknowledged. "But still he is very nice in his way, and he is so desperately fond of Joanne that I can't think why she shouldn't take him. It's such an old story by this time, however, that I suppose nothing will ever come of it. I fancy Joanne means to remain Joanne Beresford now to the end of the chapter."

"She had better do that, I should say, than marry simply because a man is in love with her," replied Godfrey bluntly.

They had turned their backs upon the house, not exactly by Mr. Helstone's wish, for each step they were taking was withdrawing them further from the other two, in whom his interest was greater than in Mrs. Travers; but Edith had never been particularly quick-sighted with regard to the feelings of other people, so she carried Godfrey about the garden, and kept him with her while she talked to him of many things. After a little while he submitted himself resignedly enough to his position. There was a sense of familiarity that touched him very keenly in this slow rambling in the fading light about these well-remembered winding walks. He would rather have had Joanne for his companion than Mrs. Travers; but he could afford to wait until another night for Joanne.

They walked about for half-an-hour, until at last a call from one of her boys took Edith from his side, and then Godfrey, left at liberty, made his way to the lawn, and found Joanne and her father sitting together there in the dusk. There was room on the bench they occupied for a third person, and Godfrey took the vacant place.

"It was just this time of year when you were here before, was it not?" the Vicar chanced to ask him after a time. "Ay, ay, I remember it was. That was a dry fine summer; it was the last one that we spent all together, before these lassies began to take flight from the old nest. And my little Femie was here then," said the Vicar quietly. "You haven't forgotten *her*, Mr. Helstone? Yes, that was the sharpest stroke God ever laid on me."

"I can well believe it," Godfrey answered with earnest sympathy.

"She was our youngest—not our *only*, but our *last*, ewe lamb. God bless her!" said the old man in a low voice.

"You must come some evening with us and see her grave," Joanne struck in after one or two moments' silence. "Hers is our only grave, you know, for poor Tom died at sea."

"Yes, *he* lies many a fathom deep," said the Vicar. "Ay, and he was a good lad too,—an upright honest lad."

"I always thought him that," replied Godfrey cordially.

After a little while their talk took a lighter tone. The two men began to recall the days they had spent with their rods together, and the Vicar held forth about the art he loved with all his old enthusiasm.

"Fish with you again? To be sure I'll fish with you again!" he told Godfrey. "When shall it be? To-morrow? Let us say to-morrow. There's nothing like taking time by the forelock."

"I quite agree with you," replied Mr. Helstone, laughing. "If you can spare the time, let us say to-morrow by all means."

"Oh, I can spare the time," said Mr. Beresford. "I've got lazy in these latter days, and the consequence of my laziness is that I've got a curate, and so that eases my back of the most part of its burden. The truth is —" and he hesitated for a moment, but after that went on very frankly, — "the truth is, Mr. Helstone, I began a good many years ago to feel that my sermons and ministrations were getting stale. I've written some fairly decent sermons in my day, but a man who can write sermons well for fifty years is a bird, it's my opinion, of rather a rare kind of plumage. So the other day I got this young fellow to come over and see if he could stir up some of our sluggish hearts a little,—and he's done

233

it, I can tell you," added the Vicar with emphasis.

"It must be a great relief to you," said Godfrey. "Fifty years of sermon-making seems certainly to me too much to be required of any one."

"I think it is," Mr. Beresford assented heartily. "It's hard on the man who makes the sermons, and harder still on the congregation who have to sit from youth to old age and listen to them. I've been sorry for *my* congregation many a day. Decent people they are too, and as patient as Job."

"I don't think they are ever likely to have been conscious that their patience was being tried," replied Godfrey, laughing.

In the dusk that had become almost night some steps sounded on the path, and Joanne said, "Here comes Violet." And then Godfrey rose, and saw a tall woman coming towards them, dressed in black.

"Yes, I remember quite well when you were here before," she said when they had shaken hands, "but it is such a long time ago. I don't think I should know your face."

Next to Lilian, Violet had been the beauty of the family; and presently, when they returned to the house and came into the light, Godfrey saw that she was very handsome still, with a finer face than Lilian's—a pale woman, with large dark eyes. In her widow's cap and long straight skirts she looked very striking, Mr. Helstone thought.

They went to their homely supper in the old way before Godfrey left them. He was given a place at table between the married sisters. He had had little all the evening to do with Joanne, but he told himself again that he could afford to wait. To-night he felt that he was only gathering up the dropped threads of former days; there was no need for haste.

"Well then, Mr. Helstone, we shall meet in the morning," the Vicar said cheerily as Godfrey took his leave at last. "I'll come to you, and we'll have a grand day of it."

"I shall feel sure of that if I have your company," Godfrey answered with warmth; and Mr. Beresford balanced himself backward on his heels and laughed.

"Ah, you are trying your hand at flattering an old man!" he exclaimed. "Well, well, we don't get wiser always as we grow in years, and the old fish, I am afraid, feels tempted to rise to the bait. Off with you, sir, and get to bed, or in the morning you'll find me before you at the river."

CHAPTER IX.

WITH talk that was sometimes gay and sometimes grave, Mr. Beresford and Godfrey passed the morning of the following day. They fished in the old pools; the weather was mild and grey; the river and the meadows, the long stretch of higher ground, the belts of wood, all looked as they had lived in Godfrey's memory for twenty years.

"Yes, Lilian left us after that summer when you were here before," the Vicar said once abruptly, "and then it was not very long after that that your own marriage came. I remember I saw it in the paper; and when she died too I saw her death. I had a mind to write to you then and say a word of sympathy; but we put off doing a vast number of things in this world, to our shame, and I put off that, till it got too late to do it. You must forgive me, sir. I've got a good sermon against dilatoriness in my study that I've preached with much gusto more than once; but, alas for us! we preach what we don't practise. It's the old story—as old as the world. We call on others to do what we fail to do ourselves."

"We had better do even that than fail to call at all," Godfrey said.

"Ay, but if the shepherd goes astray, will the sheep, do you think, go straight? Ah, I doubt it, I doubt it!" Mr. Beresford answered half aloud.

They fished till one o'clock, and then parted.

"Are you coming up this evening?" the Vicar asked; and Godfrey said—"Yes."

"That is, if you will not have had too much of me," he added next moment, upon which the Vicar laughed.

"No fear of that," he exclaimed heartily. "I've never known the day yet when a friend's face hasn't been a welcome sight."

Godfrey saw Joanne in the village after his early dinner that afternoon, and putting on his hat, for he was in the inn, ran after her and overtook her. "Are you going home?" he asked her; and when she answered "Yes," he set himself at her side. But he soon thought that he would try to make her linger a little on the way, so, after walking towards the Vicarage for a minute or two—

239

"I haven't been up to see that pretty view yet," he said abruptly, pointing towards a footpath on their left which, striking up from the road, wound through the trees to a little wooded height. "Come and let us have a look at it. You are not in a hurry, are you, to get back?"

"N—o," she replied. But she made her answer with a momentary hesitation that his ear caught.

Though his ear caught her tone, however, he took no notice of it. "I want to see it again," he merely said, and began to mount, without giving her any further opportunity to object.

He was conscious that she was not quite at ease with him, but as she followed him half unwillingly he felt little regret at that. Their companionship in these familiar spots was beset with so many recollections of former days that he knew she could not be with him now and fail to recall that other time when they had been here of old, and when he had almost been her lover.

If she was shy of him, however, his manner enabled her to gain control over her shyness soon. He had forgotten little enough that concerned those old days, but he said nothing to her of his remembrance of them as they climbed to their tiny hill-top, and stood there together, looking down on the view that he had told her he wished to see again. The place they had reached was merely a little hillock studded with trees, and the view was an ordinary one enough, though pretty and pastoral, and looking its best at this moment, for the day had improved, and the afternoon sunshine was lying brightly and softly on the hill-sides; but he had been here with Joanne before, and that fact gave a charm to the place in his eyes that, except for her remembered presence, it would not have had.

There was a felled pine tree lying on the ground, and, after they had stood still for a little while, Godfrey sat down on it.

"Are you tired?" Joanne asked when he did this.

"No; but this makes a very good seat; try it," he answered.

And then, a little reluctantly, she sat down too. She would rather not have done it perhaps, but there was a strong unwillingness in her (of which he was not unconscious) to let him see that she was unwilling.

For his part, when she took her seat at his side he was very well content. The

habit that had grown upon him through
many years had made Godfrey very
leisurely now in almost all his actions : his
blood did not flow quickly in these days ;
his resolves formed themselves rather
deliberately and steadily than with much
fervour. It gave him a keen feeling of
pleasant repose at this moment to find himself once more with Joanne Beresford as his
companion, but in this his grave middle age
he was satisfied to let his sense of the sweet
familiarity of her presence take quiet possession of him again. If he was happy to
have her near him, he had the reticence to
keep his happiness unexpressed.

He made her gradually at home with
him, and she began to talk to him very
naturally after a time. He asked her many
questions, and she answered them willingly
and frankly.

"I seem to be giving you a great deal of family history," she exclaimed once, with a laugh.

"Yes; but I am asking you for it. I am interested in you all, remember," he replied.

They talked for a long while. Perhaps they both forgot how fast the afternoon was passing. It was she who in the end was the first to look at her watch. By that time it was half-past five o'clock, and she rose up quickly from her seat.

"I shall only be home in time for tea," she said. "Are you coming with me? I mean, were you thinking of coming up to us this evening?"

"Yes," he said, "I am coming, if you will have me. I am afraid you will be asked to put up with a great deal of me, for your father has been good enough to tell

me I may come when I like; and there is
not even poor Mrs. Arthur now," he added,
" to share the burden of my company with
you."

" I don't think you ever went much to
Aunt Arthur's in the evening. She was
fashionable, and had afternoon parties, you
know," Joanne said.

He had not meant to go to the Vicarage
till tea was over, but he did not care to
deny himself the pleasure of going with
Joanne, so they walked to the house
together. He would have been content to
follow her wherever she went, for already
the old feeling was silently but surely
coming back to him which long ago had
made the place in which she was the one
in which he most desired to be.

He said something to her about her
father as they got near the Vicarage gate.

"He is the least altered of you all," he told her. "Time has touched him with a wonderfully gentle hand. I don't think he looked young for his age when I saw him first, but now he looks hale, and as if he might live for twenty more years. Yes, even *you* are more changed than he is."

"*I* must indeed be changed," she answered. "How could I fail to be? A woman may well alter between nineteen and nine-and-thirty."

"You don't look nine-and-thirty," he said quietly. "Your sister Edith is much older in appearance than you."

"Edith's stoutness has aged her," Joanne replied. "It is a pity she has got so stout, for it has changed her very much. And Lilian has grown rather stout too; but Lilian is very handsome still. And Violet is handsome; don't you think so?"

"Violet is beautiful," Godfrey answered with warmth. "I don't think your eldest sister was ever to be compared with her. One would never tire of a face like Mrs. Rawlinson's."

"No; I think that too," Joanne answered; but she spoke with the momentary sadness of a woman who, in the presence of somebody who has once loved her, remembers that her own youth is gone.

Godfrey found a stranger at the Vicarage in a long black coat.

"It is Mr. Hudson," Joanne told him. "He often comes up for a little. We like him very much—though he puts us all to shame," she added after a moment, with a little reluctance that Godfrey thought he understood. "He is doing a great deal in the parish. He works very hard," she said.

Godfrey talked to Mr Hudson a little presently, and found him wrapped up in the duties of his post—a devoted, absorbed man, indifferent to the world and the things of the world. He was a singular contrast to his Vicar, as his Vicar, with his clear good sense, very well knew.

"Yes, we are made of different stuff, Hudson and I," he said during the evening to Mr. Helstone; "but he is of the right sort. I am master and he is servant here, but we shall take different places in the next world. I always go about with him thinking that. I think it whenever we walk into church together,—I first, and he at my heels."

"Your temperaments are different," Godfrey said, "and if your temperaments are different, your lives can hardly be the same."

"Ay, but we both undertook to do our Master's work,—and he is doing it," said the old man, with a ring in his voice, "while I stand idle."

One of Violet's light-footed girls ran suddenly across their path, and the Vicar arrested her with a quick hand on her shoulder. Perhaps the diversion was not unwelcome.

"Whither away, my little lass?" he asked.

"We have lost one of our balls," the child answered. "I think it went in there."

"In there amongst the bushes? Let me see if I can find it," Godfrey said.

Before they went to supper the Vicar called for some music, and Joanne went to the piano, and sang something that Godfrey did not know. He had hoped that she would choose one of the old songs, but she did not. When she had finished he said this to her.

"I have thought so often of those old songs of yours," he said. "I hope you mean to let me hear some of them again?"

"I don't sing them often now," she answered; "but—oh yes, of course I will sing one if you like."

And then she sang one that he knew well, and it moved him as hardly anything else even had moved him yet.

He sat where he could see her well, and he listened and looked at her, with eyes that were fast getting held again by their old love, and, with every hour that passed, losing some portion of their power to perceive that time had robbed her of any charm or sweetness. It seemed to him that he had never heard a woman sing as she did; he had always thought so, even through the doubt which had sometimes crossed him, whether indeed her singing deserved the intense admiration he had given it; but now he heard it again, and the feeling with which he had listened to it of old came back to him tumultuously, with a dear familiarity. It was the emotion of twenty years ago unchanged, or, if changed at all, new only in its power to take a deeper possession of him.

She sang two songs that were sad and pathetic, and then, almost as if in mockery of their pathos, suddenly she broke into a little joyous bit of melody that rang through the room like a song from a heart that had never known a care.

"That is something else that I do not know," he said, when she had ended it; but she merely laughed at this remark as she rose up.

"Most of the songs I sing now are ones that you do not know," she said.

It was his love of fishing, he had found, that had been assumed to be one of the principal motives that had brought him back to Brentwood.

"You must be a great enthusiast," Edith had said to him; but he had laughed at that accusation.

"I pass years sometimes without taking a rod in my hand," he assured her. "Oh no, I have no claim to be called an enthusiast; I am simply a man at this moment who has lost his moorings."

"And have you come here to recover them?" asked Edith in her old sharp way. "I beg your pardon! I am very sorry for you,—only it seems odd."

"I have come here because you all made me happy amongst you long ago," Godfrey said. "I am idle, and I like to ramble about your woods and by your river. I have not many old friends, and so I like to renew my hold upon the few I possess."

"Well, that's very nice; and if I may look upon myself as one of the old friends, I feel grateful," Edith answered cordially.

Godfrey liked Mrs. Travers for the sake of former days, and now in these present ones he gave himself up to be talked to by her a good deal. She was staying here with her boys during her husband's absence from home for a few weeks, and about both her husband and her children, and indeed about most other things in heaven and earth, she seemed to take a lively pleasure in conversing with Mr. Helstone. Violet was generally rather shy and reserved with him, but Edith treated him with the frankest friendliness.

"I wish you had seen Vi at her best," she said to him one day. "She *was* a pretty creature. But she is awfully changed now. Doesn't she look ill and sad? You see, hers was a complete love-match, and I am sure I don't wonder at it, for Fred Rawlinson was simply delightful. When he died it was something dreadful for her."

"I think Mrs. Rawlinson is wonderfully handsome still," Godfrey answered. "It is really a noble face."

"Well, I am glad you think so," said Edith heartily. "I always thought her beautiful myself, even when she was only a little thing. And do you remember how

Mr. Dallas used to admire her, and say he would come back to marry her? Well, he has been a good while in marrying anybody, and I suppose now his wife isn't much like Violet?"

"She is not indeed," Godfrey answered with a laugh. "Though some of us who love her think her pretty enough, I am afraid she couldn't hold a candle to Mrs. Rawlinson."

"Ah, well, we can't all be beauties," said Edith philosophically. "I was never very pretty myself, and I am awfully fat now; but if I were as handsome as the best of them, I don't think I could be a bit happier. For I am *very* happy, Mr. Helstone. I don't envy any woman either her face or her fortune. There is Lilian, for instance; I'm sure, though she is twice as rich as we are, I wouldn't change places with *her* for millions; and here is poor Violet, with her husband dead,—and Joanne, who has never had a husband at all. There is none of them so well off as I am,—not one, in spite of them all being so much better-looking than I ever pretended to be;" and Mrs. Travers complacently caressed her plump white hands, and then looked up into Godfrey's face with a laugh.

"You are thinking that self-satisfaction is a very bad thing, aren't you?" she asked him. "Oh, well, I know it is. But contentment isn't a bad thing, nor gratitude to God and the people who have made one happy. And I am sure I don't mean that I *deserve* to be happier than the rest of them; I only mean that I *am* happier, and that I think I have got the best husband amongst them all."

"And do *you* too prefer Mr. Travers to

your other brothers-in-law?" Godfrey asked Joanne one day after this.

But Joanne looked rather amused, and—

"Has Edith been telling you that he is better than the rest?" she said. "Well, *she* believes he is, of course, and they are very happy together, and he is really very nice, in a way. But I think it is rather a commonplace way. You wouldn't care much for him, I am afraid. Oh no," she added after a moment, "Fred Rawlinson was the brother-in-law I cared for most."

"Mr. Rawlinson seems to have been very fortunate," Godfrey said. "He won golden opinions apparently all round."

"Yes—we all liked him," Joanne answered, —"every one of us. It was a great pleasure to us when he asked Vi to marry him, and it was a great—it was a *very* great—sorrow to us when he died."

"Then you and he were friends?" Godfrey said abruptly.

"Yes—we were great friends," she answered

CHAPTER X.

In these pleasant idle days, when Godfrey was leading the same life again that he had led in that other unforgotten holiday so many years ago, a considerable part of his time soon came to be spent with Joanne. He was at the Vicarage during some part of every four-and-twenty hours. As it had been of old, he became again almost one of themselves, coming and going as he liked. He often went fishing with the Vicar; he made friends with the new generation of children; he talked a great deal with Edith, and a little with Violet,

259

but most of all he cared to be where Joanne was.

She was fond of walking, and as often as it was possible he used to accompany her on her walks. At first he tried to give an appearance of chance to these meetings with her, but presently he ventured gradually to let her see that they did not come by chance. One day he found her sitting sketching, and as he threw himself down on the grass beside her he told her frankly that he was delighted to know that he should be able to find her in this same spot on future days.

"For this drawing will take you a long time to do, I hope?" he said.

"That will depend upon how I do it, I suppose," she answered — a little consciously perhaps.

"Then do it carefully and minutely,"

he said. "I don't like the Impressionist school of art. When I look at a tree in a picture I like to be able to count its leaves."

"I am sure you don't," she replied laughing.

But he proceeded to read her a lecture gravely on the necessity for deliberation and completeness in her work, and would not allow that he was talking in jest.

She made her picture that day, and he lay at her feet with a feeling of supreme content. His life since he had been here last seemed to be fading away from him in these happy weeks,—all growing dim in the charm of this recovered atmosphere that was giving him back his youth and the hope that he had lost so long ago. He often now almost forgot that neither he nor she was young; she seemed so little changed; he felt so little changed too.

He was thinking this to-day, when, curiously, in the midst of his thoughts, she began suddenly to speak about that life that he had left behind him.

She had never done this until now; the briefest reference to the past, and to Margaret, had been all that had ever passed between them. But perhaps she had already had it in her mind to break her silence; for to-day, after there had been a pause for a minute or two between them, she all at once began to speak, in a way that did not seem to be unpremeditated.

"May I say something to you?" she asked abruptly, and rather nervously. "You know, after that day—long ago—when I saw you last—of course I often thought about your marriage. I often wondered if you were content." She hesitated for a moment. "I have no right to ask—but—

you *were* content, were you not ? " she said timidly.

" Yes—I was content," he deliberately replied.

He made no other answer for a minute ; but at the end of that time he began to speak again, very gravely.

" You helped me that day when I needed help," he said. " God knows I have all my life been grateful to you.—No, I never repented my marriage. My wife was one of the best and most unselfish of women,— and she never knew—what I went that day in my trouble and told to *you*. That was best—wasn't it ? "

" I knew you wouldn't tell her," Joanne said quickly. " It was only to keep silent for a little while—till her love made you love her."

" Well—I did that," he answered. " You

gave me strength to do it. So I have owed not a little to you, you see.—Oh no, I have not been an unhappy man. She gave her whole life to me for seventeen years, poor girl; and she gave me Rita too. My little daughter was a great consolation to me."

"I never knew whether you had any children until that day I saw you at Mrs. Lomas's. I used often to wonder if you had," Joanne said.

"After your goodness to me perhaps I might have told you. Did you think I might?" he asked. "Well, it was not want of gratitude to you, at any rate, that kept me silent."

And then there was a pause, which seemed to come abruptly, for he had asked her a question, but she had not answered it.

"The worst is that when the end comes

we regret so many things," he said, beginning to speak again, after a minute or more
had passed in silence. "While opportuni-
ties are ours we do so little, and then comes
the 'too late' that stops it all."

"Yes; but if you made her happy—"
she said, hesitating a little.

"You assume that I made her happy,"
he interrupted her. "I am afraid if she
was happy it was only her own goodness
that made her so,—not mine. Mine to her
was poor enough,—a negative goodness at
the best, that took all she gave me (which
was her life and her every thought), and
returned her only enough affection to make
me simply kind. That is not much to
boast of. It is a poor thing to be all that
I can say."

"But *she* would have said more perhaps,"
Joanne answered quickly.

"Very possibly, for she was the sort of woman to magnify small things. But the truth is as I put it, Miss Beresford," Godfrey returned abruptly, with almost harsh decision. "I tell you so,—and I can only ask you to find an excuse for me, if you think an excuse exists."

And then she made no answer. "The light is changing so; I think I shall have to stop," she only said after a little silence; and then he rose and came to look at what she had been doing.

She had covered her paper with colour, and he shook his head at her.

"You are generalizing far too much. I call this a very hasty blotty style," he told her. "At this rate, after another two hours' work, you will call your picture finished, and *I* shall not be able to discover one finished bit in it from end to end."

"Not so much as a single tree with its leaves defined!" she said laughing.

"A single tree! I shall not find so much as a single twig! And yet—if it will not make you vain—I confess," he allowed, "that there seems to me something in this. You couldn't have done it, I imagine, when I was here before."

"I may well have improved a little in all these years," she said. "I have had lessons since you were here."

"And you had always a natural gift for it, I think," he answered. "Yes—even when you drew much less well than you do now I used to like your sketches. Do you remember one day when I came upon you drawing in the wood above the river?"

"Yes; I remember it," she said.

"You let me stay with you that day too. You were doing some birch trees.

267

I wonder if you have got that drawing still?"

"I never finished it," she said a little quickly. "I was only beginning it that day."

"Well, I had thought it was worth finishing," he merely replied.

They had been used to play croquet in those other evenings at the Vicarage: they played tennis now, but it was for the most part only the children who played. The others, whose age for games was past, merely looked on. But yet Godfrey found these evenings no less pleasant to him than those others had been when he was young.

There were seats on the large lawn where they could sit and talk; they had the garden to ramble about, and the adjacent fields, which they entered by the wicket gate that led down to the river, to turn into if they wanted to extend their walk. Very often Mr. Beresford and Joanne and Godfrey strolled down across these meadows to the river to see the sun set. It was in these fields that Godfrey had seen Joanne first. He well remembered the very spot where he had been standing with his rod when he turned round and found her coming towards him.

"And your arrival put me out, because I had been about to wade in after that hat of mine," he told her one evening, laughing.

"We were quite unconscious that we put you out—and after all, you see, we saved you the trouble of wading," she answered.

"Yes," he said, "you did the first of your good deeds to me that day." And then he added—"You have done many a one since."

One evening when the Vicar and Mr.

Helstone happened to be alone (they were out of doors, and for the moment all the others had dispersed in different directions), Godfrey, yielding to a sudden impulse, said something to him about Joanne. Mr. Beresford had chanced to make a passing remark about her.

"Joanne generally has a trick of being more right than the rest of them," he said.

Upon which Godfrey made the abrupt answer—

"I think she is always right. This world would cease to be imperfect at all if all women in it were like her."

"Ay?" said the Vicar briskly upon this, and his eyes sent out rather a sharp glance on his companion.

And then Godfrey went on deliberately—"I have always thought so—almost from the first day I ever knew her."

They were walking together round the garden, and an abrupt silence followed these last words. Godfrey hardly knew why he had spoken them; he hardly knew after a minute why he spoke again. But it was at least a generous feeling that made him do it,—a sudden feeling of pity and sympathy for the old man, whose dearest possession he had set his heart on taking from him.

"Mr. Beresford, I think you must know why I am here," he abruptly said. "Twenty years ago, if it had been in my power, I would have asked Joanne to be my wife."

"And—lad! have you come back to ask her now?" said the Vicar, almost with a cry. There was a momentary fire in his face,—a sudden wrath that made his eyes flash, and gave him the look of an old soldier facing his foe. But the flame hardly lasted more than a second. "I might have known," he added almost immediately, in a tone that had fallen into another key. "I am an old fool—for I might have known."

"She is more dear to me than I can trust myself to tell you," Godfrey said in a low voice, for he was trying to control an emotion that almost got the mastery of him. "She was the love of my youth, but she is dearer to me now even than she was in those old days—though both her youth and mine are gone. If I take her from you—"

"So you think she'll have you?" the Vicar interrupted him wistfully. He looked at Godfrey for a moment. "Ah, well—you know about it probably," he added with an effort,—"and I have an old man's dim eyes and have not seen." He was silent for a few seconds; then in a low voice—"My poor lass!" he said; "and did *she* think of this too twenty years ago?"

"I never had the right to ask her that," Godfrey answered, with a keenness of memory that sent the hot blood to his face.

The Vicar walked on quickly a little way ahead of his companion. They were near the gate that led into the meadow, and when he reached it he opened it and passed through.

"One can breathe better here," he said as Godfrey followed him, "and a man feels the need of a deep breath at times. You see, sir, you have given me a blow."

"I am afraid I have," Godfrey answered quickly; "and you will find it hard to forgive me for it."

"Nay, nay, sir!" cried the old man vigorously, "that is a thing you need not fear. About forgiveness you have no call to speak. As I say, this—this shakes me a little, you understand,—but God forbid that I should grudge her any happiness. I have never done that, I trust. I would cut my right hand off and fling it in the fire rather than do it now !"

With a ring in his voice he took his hat from his head. They had been standing still, but suddenly he began to stride towards the river. For a few moments Godfrey looked after him, doubtful whether to follow him or not ; then he turned back again towards the still open gate. " Where is Joanne ? " he was thinking to himself.

He went back into the garden and approached the house, looking for her. The usual stir of young voices was in the air, and the children with Edith were on the lawn, preparing for their customary pastime. Joanne he found presently sitting with her mother by one of the open drawing-room windows. It was not a French window, but one with a low sill on which those who were out of doors, if they wished to talk to the occupants of the room, could come and lean or sit. Godfrey had often come and leant there before this. He stood now for a good while talking to the two women within.

The click of Mrs. Beresford's knitting needles mingled with the sound of their voices. She knitted socks for her grandsons now, as she had knitted for an earlier generation twenty years ago.

"You must have made a great many pairs in your life," Godfrey said, watching her work, at a pause in their talk.

"They have *worn out* a great many pairs," the old lady answered with alacrity. "You would scarcely believe it, I dare say, Mr. Helstone, but I can hardly make them fast enough. I can't knit now as fast as I did, you see," and she shook her head. "One's fingers get stiff as they grow old."

"They may well be stiff with all the work they have done—dear old fingers," Joanne said tenderly, and stooped and put her lips on them.

But Mrs. Beresford went on with her knitting unmoved by the caress. She had never been a demonstrative woman, and perhaps she thought less of Joanne than she did of some of her other daughters, because she had had Joanne with her all her life.

She thought less of her than she did of Violet, Godfrey thought, when presently Mrs. Rawlinson came into the room, and her mother, at her entrance, let her stocking for a few moments lie upon her lap.

"My dear, I had been wondering what you were doing?" she said, looking up at her.

"I was only in my room. Did you want me?" Violet answered. And then she took a seat by her mother's side.

"I didn't want you particularly, child, but I always like to know where you are," Mrs. Beresford said.

"It is such a pleasant evening. Can you come out a little?" Godfrey asked Joanne a few minutes afterwards, and she answered "Yes," and joined him outside.

"What have you done with papa? I thought you were together?" she had already inquired.

"We were together, but he left me,' he replied.

She did not guess as she joined Godfrey in the garden that he wanted her to-night more than (perhaps she knew) he always wanted her.

"It is nice out here. The drawing-room was very hot," she merely said.

"So I thought," he answered. "I wanted to get you out of it. Come away; let us turn our backs upon them all."

"Where do you want to go to?" she asked him; but when he answered to this —"Where I can have you to myself,"— then she made no reply.

These two had been together now for three or four weeks, in a companionship that had grown gradually and almost daily closer and more intimate. But Joanne perhaps had come to think that it was rather the intimacy of warm friends than lovers, — an intimacy that had reached a certain point, and would rest there. "You are the best woman I have ever known,"

278

he told her once. "When I want an ideal of sweet womanhood I think of *you*." But in general he did not make speeches of this kind to her; he had made her conscious that he felt something for her that he felt for no one else; but she knew he had loved her once, and, remembering that, she scarcely thought he loved her now.

There were two paths across the meadows, one leading to the river, one to other fields in which the corn was ripening. "Let us go this way," he said, and turned from the river to the right, and in a little while they reached those yellowing crops. There was a gate here, and she would have passed through it, but at this point he stopped her.

"Suppose we go no farther. I like a gate to lean on. We are very well here," he said, and folded his arms upon the

279

upper rail. Then she stood still too. The wind was passing lightly over the corn. There was a breezy sky, with torn clouds in the west.

She said, after they had talked for a few minutes—

"Do you remember in the old time that we came and stood at this gate once before, —my father, and you, and I?—and we talked about painters, and what they could make of this kind of country?"

"And your father stood here, and you on the other side of him," he replied. "Yes—I remember it. You stood with your hand in his arm. I can see you now in your light dress, and with your young face. And I stood here," he added suddenly, "envying the touch that you were giving to some one else."

"Shall we not walk on?" she abruptly

asked, and put her hand upon the fastening of the gate. Both his words and his tone had made the colour come to her face. But he shook his head.

"No—why should we walk on? We will stay here and talk," he answered. "I want to go on talking about those days. Do you not know what they were to me?—There is a thing I want you to tell me frankly." He paused for a moment, and then looked straight at her and put his question.

"Did you know that I loved you when I was here before?"

She turned her face hurriedly away from him; she said nothing for a moment or two; then she answered in a low voice—"I did not *know* it."

"You were not sure of it, you mean?" he replied at once. "But you *were* sure—

you *did* know it, before the end—on that day when I saw you last?"

"Yes—I knew it then," she said.

She made her answer steadily, but the next moment she suddenly changed her position, and—

"Why should we talk of it?" she said nervously. "Better not. All that is so long ago."

"But I have you with me again," he quickly answered, "and, suppose it is long ago, what then? Do you think that that summer when I knew you first does not stand out for me from all the other summers of my life? If it had been possible for me to have spoken to you at the end of those happy weeks,—my dear, would you have sent me away? Perhaps I have no right to ask you, but—as you said just now—it is so long ago, and you may trust me enough to tell me, I think?"

"Do I not know that I may trust you? Have I not trusted you always?" she answered, with a little thrill in her voice. And then after only a moment or two's silence—"If I had not done that, and if you had not come to me that last day," she said half aloud, "I think my life would have been very different. But that day made everything almost easy to bear."

"*My* Joanne!" he said.

Her answer perhaps had given him the right to claim her as he did. Her hand was on the gate, and he put his own firmly above it. But they stood after this without speaking, till presently she was the first to break the silence.

"I have said this," she began, in a low voice that trembled a little; "but you

must not misunderstand me. You must
not think that because of those old days
I have been an unhappy woman, for it is
not so. There was never anything to regret
in those days, nor, as far as I was concerned,
in the consequences of them. I did not—
care to marry afterwards; that was all; but
I have had a happy life. You must believe
me when I tell you that."

"I do believe it," he answered quietly.
" But—now ?" he added after a moment's
silence.

"Now we are friends again,—and you
are here again," she said with a quiver in
her voice,—"and I am very glad."

She suddenly tried to move away, but
he tightened his hand over hers and
stopped her.

"You must not go," he said. " What
have we two to do apart? I want you to

feel, as I do, that it brings back your youth for us to be together again."

She smiled, but she half shook her head.

"You are a man," she said. "You are younger than I am now."

"Do you mean by that to tell me that you are too old to care for me?" he asked.

"Oh no!" she said quickly; "not that. I only meant—" and then she dropped her voice suddenly, "that I am too old to be cared for."

"Joanne!" he said passionately.

It was a lover's call to her, let her be young or old; and she looked at him for one moment,—and then, whatever else she might have meant to say, was never said, and she only flushed like a girl, and held her peace.

The distant country had grown dim, and the trees were almost black against the sky as they walked back presently across the fields. "They will wonder where we have been," Joanne said, shy at the thought of the confession that she had to make. But Godfrey opened the gate that led them back into the garden, caring little enough for that.

There was a lamp burning inside the hall at the house, and through the open door as they came towards it a little stream of light fell on the Vicar's figure standing alone upon the gravel walk. Joanne went up to him with her heart beating fast, and put her hands about his arm.

"Well, my lass?" he quietly said.

He could not see her face, but Godfrey spoke abruptly and eagerly. "She has been the best of all your daughters," he said,—"the dearest and best." And then the old man gave a laugh that sounded rather sad and cold beside the other's warmth.

"Ay, ay," he answered, "there have been others before you who have told me that."

He drew her close to him for a few moments, and she began suddenly to cry upon his breast; but at the sound of her weeping the brave old man in a moment straightened himself.

"My dear, we must have no tears," he said quickly, with the customary cheery tone again in his mellow voice. "You only mean to tell me that you are going to marry this fellow, I suppose? Well, God bless me, that's no matter for tears, I hope? He's a likely fellow enough, as it seems to me, though"—with a laugh--"he has appeared a little late in the season, one might say, perhaps. And, for my own part, I've been blest with a good sprinkling of sons-in-law already, and I'm bound to allow I'm rather the better for them than the worse. So, Mr. Helstone, in spite of this being a little unexpected, here's my hand, and you can take Joanne's along with it. And now," said the Vicar briskly, " in with you both, and let us tell our news to the old wife."

THE END.

CLAY AND TAYLOR, PRINTERS, BUNGAY, SUFFOLK.   G. C. & Co.